D0801599

Also by Tony Abbott

Firegirl
The Postcard

LUNCH-BOX DREAM

Tony Abbott

FRANCES FOSTER BOOKS
FARRAR STRAUS GIROUX
NEW YORK

Copyright © 2011 by Tony Abbott
All rights reserved
Distributed in Canada by D&M Publishers, Inc.
Printed in June 2011 in the United States of America
by RR Donnelley & Sons Company, Harrisonburg, Virginia
Designed by Jay Colvin
First edition, 2011
1   3   5   7   9   10   8   6   4   2

mackids.com

Library of Congress Cataloging-in-Publication Data
Abbott, Tony.
    Lunch-box dream / Tony Abbott. — 1st ed.
    p.   cm.
    Summary: Told from multiple point of view, a white family on a 1959 road trip between Ohio and Florida, visiting Civil War battlefields along the way, crosses paths with a black family near Atlanta, where one of their children has gone missing.
    ISBN: 978-0-374-34673-7
    [1. Voyages and travels—Fiction.   2. Segregation—Fiction. 3. Race relations—Fiction.   4. Family life—Fiction.   5. Missing children—Fiction.   6. African Americans—Fiction.   7. Southern States—History—1951-   —Fiction.]   I. Title.

PZ7.A1587Lun 2011
[Fic]—dc22

                                              2010033105

Grandmother, Mother, Brother
1978, 2009, 2006

Lunch in a Jim Crow Car

Get out the lunch-box of your dreams.
Bite into the sandwich of your heart,
And ride the Jim Crow car until it screams
Then—like an atom bomb—it bursts apart.
    —*Langston Hughes*

LUNCH-BOX DREAM

CAST OF CHARACTERS

Cleveland
Bobby
Ricky, *Bobby's older brother*
Marion, *their mother*
Grandma, *their grandmother*

Atlanta
Louisa Thomas (Weeza)
Jacob Thomas, *Louisa's younger brother, age nine*
Hershel Thomas, *Louisa's husband*
Ruth Vann, *Hershel and Frank's mother*
Ellis Vann, *Hershel's stepfather*
James and Jimmy Sharp, *residents of the city*

Dalton
Frank Thomas, *Hershel's brother*
Olivia Thomas, *Frank's wife*
Cora Baker, *Olivia's younger sister, age fifteen*
Irene and Albert Baker, *Olivia and Cora's parents*

One of the men began to hum,
then hum with his mouth open, then sing.

Thursday, June 11, 1959

ONE

Bobby

They called them chocolate men, Bobby and his brother.

You didn't see them on the East Side, high over Euclid, except once or twice a week and only early in the morning.

Where did they come from? There were no chocolate boys and girls in his school or at church. There were no chocolate ladies living in his neighborhood. There were no chocolate families at the park or the outdoor theater or the ball field. And yet the men came every week to his house.

That morning, as he lay on the grass by the sidewalk, Bobby heard them coming again.

First there was the roar and squeal of the big truck. That was far up the street. It was early, the time when the sun edged over the rooftops, but warm for the middle of June. Bobby was sharpening Popsicle sticks into little knives while his brother watched.

"Hurry up," Ricky said.

Or not, thought Bobby. You have to do this properly. To sharpen a stick correctly you scraped it slantways against the sidewalk seams, and it took a while. With each stroke, you drew the stick toward you or pushed it away from you in a curving motion, like a barber stropping his razor in a Western movie.

Bobby wanted a thin blade, and his cheek was right down there above the sidewalk, with one eye squeezed shut to focus on the motion of his hand. The concrete scratched his knuckles, whited his skin, but you had to do it that way. You needed to scrape the stick nearly flat against the sidewalk to give you the thinnest blade.

Bobby would use the knife for little things. It could be a tool, or a weapon in a soldier game; it might be used to carve modeling clay, or as a casually found stick that on the utterance of a secret phrase became a lost cutlass of legend; or as a makeshift sidearm for defense on the schoolyard; or as nothing much, a thing to stab trees with or to jab into the ground to unearth bugs and roots or to press against your pocketed palm as you walked through stores downtown.

If his mother found one, she tossed it away.

Or he suspected she did. He had seen his sticks

snapped in half in the wastebasket and he didn't think his brother threw them there. It was Ricky who had taught him how to shape the knives, though he didn't make them himself anymore. And it wasn't their father, because he was hardly home these days.

"Hurry up," Ricky said.

"This one will be good," said Bobby, taking his time to get the sharpest edge. "Maybe my best."

The truck moved, then stopped, then moved and stopped closer. The boys looked up. They watched the chocolate men jump off the sides of the truck. The ash cans were loud when they scraped them over the sidewalk and into the street, dragging them with leathery hands. Their yelling was not like the sound of the brown men and women who sang and played pianos on television. They approached, crisscrossing the sidewalk.

"That's it," said Ricky. "I don't want to be here when they come. I'm going in."

Bobby scooped up his knives, and the two boys ran inside. Ricky, a year older, was faster. They pulled the living room drapes aside and through the big window saw their cans being scraped and lifted.

"That one guy's huge."

"Did you see that? He took both Downings' cans at the same time."

Thick bare brown arms raised and shook the cans, the truck swallowed the trash, the cans were swung back and set down, and the men were on to the next house and the next. The boys watched from the picture window until the men disappeared down Cliffview to wherever they had come from.

"Let's go out back," said Ricky.

"I want to watch TV," Bobby said.

"No, let's go out back. I have a tennis ball."

"Bring the cans into the carport, please," said their mother. "Then breakfast. I have something to tell you."

"In a minute, Mom," Ricky called. To Bobby he said: "Let's go out back first."

"Yeah, okay."

TWO

"We're going to drive Grandma home," their mother said after she found them in the backyard and shooed them into the kitchen.

Ricky looked up from his plate of French toast. He pushed his glasses to the bridge of his nose and blinked. "What, where?"

"Grandma. Home," she said.

Their mother was tall and slim, still young, and wore a print summer dress and sandals. As she spoke, she leaned back against the counter with the sink behind her. She smelled of lotion and egg batter and cinnamon, and her face was strained.

"We're going to drive Grandma home to Florida."

Bobby glanced over at his grandmother. She was sitting at the table between him and his brother, but talk often floated around her as if she wasn't there. She was Hungarian. Her accent was heavy and her

English was slow and odd. She had come over from Hungary in the 1920s and said "vindshield vipers."

"Drive?" Bobby said, licking his fork and wondering what lay behind his mother's expression. Was it something he had done? Not coming in when she first called? Or hadn't he heard her on the phone that morning? Had his father said something to upset her? "Will our car even make it all the way?" he asked. "It stalls a lot. And smells when it rains—"

"No, not Suzabelle," she said. "Not our car. We're driving Grandma's car. She wants it down there with her."

Bobby looked at Grandma longer this time. Her eyes were trained on his mother. Grandma's face was pouchy, wrinkled, hollowed since he'd last seen her months ago, and strange to kiss, like kissing a soft cloth bag, as he had to do every bedtime. Her skin was olive like the circles he noticed under his mother's eyes. Was that a Hungarian thing? Would he get them, too?

"It's good on the road," his mother said. "The Chrysler."

Bobby had nearly forgotten about the big green car. It had been parked around the corner for three weeks doing nothing because no one drove it. They called it Grandma's car, but Grandma didn't really drive it. She didn't know how to drive.

"All the way?" said Ricky. He sat back in his

chair, away from the table, as if ready to talk in place of their father. "It's a thousand miles, you know. A thousand miles from here to Florida by car."

Chuckling, Bobby thought to himself: It's a thousand miles by buses and trains, too! Or maybe not, he thought. Ricky studied maps and knew distances, so maybe not.

"Probably close to thirteen hundred miles, depending on your route . . ." Ricky added, so Bobby guessed he really did know how far it was.

"Yes, I know," said their mother, pulling a narrow spiral-bound notebook out of a stack of papers on the counter, "but we're going to make a vacation of it. And on the way . . ."—she let her eyes float from Ricky to Bobby and back—". . . we're going to stop at battlefields. The Civil War battlefields in Kentucky, Tennessee, Georgia—"

"Battlefields?" Ricky dropped his fork on his plate and roared. "Are you kidding? Battlefields? Yes! Mom! Yes!" He jumped from the table and stomped up and down loudly on the kitchen floor. "Georgia? The Atlanta Campaign! Chickamauga! Yes! And yes! And yes!"

"Richie—" said his grandmother. "Please—"

Battlefields, thought Bobby. He wondered if his grandmother knew what they were. What did she know about the Civil War? He looked at her face now that it was turned toward his brother. She was old, but he didn't know how old. Seventy? Eighty? Then he remembered his mother had told him she was born in the first year of the century. So she was fifty-nine. Was that still old?

Grandma had arrived three weeks ago, after being driven by a friend from Florida to visit Grandpa's grave in Youngstown. They had then continued on to Cleveland, leaving Grandma and her car with them at their house on Cliffview Road. Grandpa had died four months before.

It was Bobby's first death.

That was something.

THREE

The story was that Grandpa had a heart attack trying to lift his car out of a sandbank. It happened in Florida on a newly opened bridge, which he had wanted to see because he was an engineer and had designed bridges when he was younger.

Bobby had been told that during the Depression his grandfather was paid with canned fruit instead of money, and he wondered what kind of bridge you built if you only got peaches for it.

Grandpa was sixty-six years old and had retired with Grandma to Florida the previous July, had enjoyed his house for seven months, had visited bridges, had not even gotten around to changing his Ohio license plates, and then was dead.

Bobby had glimpsed him, briefly, in his coffin at the family service in Youngstown. His sharp white nose, straight lips, and colorless, unmoving hands. His thin-rimmed spectacles over closed eyes.

"Richie, sit," Grandma said, patting the straw place mat next to her. "Finish your French toast. Come and sit, please."

Ricky didn't. Not wanting to see her face as Ricky went on dancing, Bobby bent his head to the plate and dug into his toast.

As he ate, he remembered his mother telling him that a gravestone had been cut with the names and birth dates of both his grandparents, and his grandfather's death date, but that it hadn't been finished before Grandma needed to return home.

Last month his mother had told him: "This summer is the first time Grandma can arrange for someone to drive with her from Florida to Youngstown to see the finished stone on the grave."

"But he's in there, right?" asked Bobby.

"In there . . . ?"

"He's been in the grave since he died, right?"

"Of course! It's just that it took time to carve the stone, and Grandma couldn't wait for it." She had paused, frowning, then added, "Bobby, of course he's there."

He now imagined two or three men jabbing at the dirt hard as iron, their shovel blades pinging a few times, then looking up to meet the eyes of the man whose job it was to see they did the work right.

Did chocolate men dig graves? Did they dig the holes for everyone, no matter what color they were, because other people wouldn't do it? Bare brown arms shoveling. Or no. It was February in Youngstown. Coats and gloves.

"We're going to take the long way around," his mother continued, flapping the notebook in her hand. "I already know how we'll drive. They made up a TripTik for me at the Triple-A—"

"Can I see it?" asked Ricky.

She handed him the notebook bound at the top with a coil of black plastic. "Five, maybe six days driving down. Through Kentucky and Tennessee and Georgia, then a day or two in St. Pete, then back—"

"But wait," said Bobby. "How will we get home? How will we come back if we leave the car with Grandma?" He had just thought of this. "We're not taking the bus home, are we? There are always chocolate people on the bus when we go downtown. And they . . . Is it really a thousand miles? On the bus? Not on the bus—"

Her smile tightened, and she shook her head.

"No. And I don't like to hear you call them that, Bobby. After we leave the car with Grandma we'll fly home from Tampa. Your first airplane, boys. How would that be?"

"Yes! Yes!" said Ricky, twirling on his heels again, up and down the floor. "This is so neat!"

"Richie, please sit."

"Fly home?" said Bobby, barely able to keep in his chair, either, and smiling at his mother now to show he was sorry for calling them that. "We'll fly home? Really, Mom? A plane? You promise?"

Taking her eyes off Ricky, his mother smiled warmly at him. Everything was all right now. She wasn't mad anymore. "In a plane, absolutely," she said. "That okay, Bobby?"

If they had to be mushed together in the car, all four of them for a week, in order to fly on an airplane, it might be okay.

"I think *so*!" he said.

FOUR

Every second since, Bobby had to hear his brother sing the strange music of those names.

"Chickamauga!" Ricky said, accentuating the "mawwww" of the word. "Shiloh, Chattanooga, Allatoona Pass, Kennesaw Mountain, Missionary Ridge!"

To Bobby the names sounded of the deep past.

Something dark lived in them, like the blurry old photographs in Ricky's books, and he certainly wouldn't go around saying the names as if they were cereal brands or car makes. The words might conjure ghosts out of ditches, from rutted paths, or the long roads that browned away into the distance in those old pictures. He imagined sunken folds in the earth, culverts, Ricky called them, that you tumbled into after nightfall when your pistol misfired and you lost your soul and your friends forgot they ever knew you.

"The year after next will be the really big year," Ricky said, flopping onto his bed with his Civil War atlas. They were alone now, their mother stepping out to drive the car up into the driveway to "air out," while their grandmother slid off to the den where she slept with the door open. "The centenary is still two years away," he said, "but I know they're restoring the battlefields for tourists already. The newspapers are full of stuff. They have to be ready. Two years is nothing."

Ricky stacked three large books in the suitcase sprawled open on his bed and kept one to look through. It was a book of photographs and prints of the Atlanta Campaign.

"We'll drive right here," he said, turning the book around and holding it up so Bobby could see the page, then tapping his finger on a scratchy brown photograph of ruined buildings. "Right here," he said, as the same finger slid across the photo to what looked like a mound of bodies rolling by in a blurry wagon. "Can you believe it? Right where it happened." He twisted the book back to himself. "It's so neat."

"Yeah," said Bobby.

When he had turned seven, Ricky had asked for an atlas. Their father had bought it happily; their

father, who was now at college in Washington, studying to be a history teacher—professor, it turned out,
when Bobby understood it. Since receiving the
atlas, Ricky had spent hours redrawing many county
and state borders with his collection of colored pencils. He had sketched in the lines of opposing armies,
great curved arrows converging with other-colored
arrows on some miserable landmark. Once, Bobby
pulled the atlas from the bookcase when Ricky was
in the backyard and saw where his brother had re-
cast the standard outlines of states with dotted lines
of permanent ink. Circles appeared around minor
towns; these represented the sites of imaginary battles. Casualty counts were scribbled in pencil up and
down the margins of the pages. Horrific numbers,
under the headings CSA and USA. Thousands upon
thousands. Bobby couldn't imagine how high the
numbers were. Was this how many men died in war?

"Okay," said Bobby. "But how long has it been?
Since the Civil War?"

"In years, months, or days?"

"You dope," said Bobby.

Ricky snickered. "The war started in 1861. I
keep telling you that. What do you think 'centenary' means? The Rebels shelled Fort Sumter on
April 12, 1861."

"Shelled? You mean—"

"Fired shells at. Cannons. That was the beginning. Armies spread out after that, all over the South."

"And stuff is happening at the battlefields now?"

"Look." Ricky unfolded a creased clipping of yellow newspaper that he slipped from inside one of the books in his suitcase. The headline read: "Civil War Battlefields Tour: Two Weeks of Leisurely Driving Through Famous National Shrines." The article was dated April 5, 1953, and had been saved a long time by their father before he gave it to Ricky, who then kept it pressed between the pages of the atlas. The paper was browned at its edges and stiff. Ricky held up the map that accompanied the article. It was labeled "Highways to American History."

"And because most of the fighting was in the South," he said, "there are lots of battlefields to visit."

"Because the South lost," said Bobby, pulling his own red suitcase out from under his bed.

"That doesn't have anything to do with it," Ricky said, sounding annoyed. "It's because most of the fighting was down there. I told you that, too. The real big northern battle is Gettysburg, Pennsylvania, but we won't be going that way. But some of the best are on the way to where Grandma lives. Even Kentucky has a couple. But Tennessee and Georgia, oh boy."

Bobby didn't care so much, except that he was supposed to care. It was battlefields. The bluecoats and the graycoats. Cannon blasts and cavalry. Swords and pistols and flying bullets. You were supposed to want to walk around where so many fought and died.

Ricky had already taken two shelves of their small bookcase for the Civil War. Worst of all were the collections of photographs their father had bought for him: bodies lying in fields, bodies in shadowy dens, bodies stacked next to one another near fences, bloated and unreal, their hips twisted the way they fell, their stiff hands reaching to touch something that wasn't there. Did shovelers break those hands and arms and legs to get them into coffins? Bobby imagined the sound of snapping bone, the pop of swollen flesh. Or did they dig oversize graves and just shove the dead, body after body, into the trenches? Did chocolate men dig graves back then, too? Didn't they have to, if someone told them to? Wasn't the war about them?

"We're going to see all these fields. Lookout Mountain, Chattanooga. Chickamauga is huge and right near Lookout Mountain," Ricky said. "Kennesaw Mountain is outside Atlanta, which we're driving through." He started to breathe over his pictures.

"Neat," said Bobby, slowly opening his drawer of the dresser and looking inside at the folded clothes.

"As long as we don't have to take the bus. Chocolate people always sit behind you."

"We won't," his brother said. "But that's how they all come here."

"What do you mean? On the bus?"

Ricky didn't look at him. "Clam up and let me read."

Friday, June 12

FIVE

Louisa

Jacob rode the bus from Atlanta north to Dalton this morning. He left with my husband Hershel. Then Hershel will come back home and Jacob will stay in Dalton.

It will only be for one week.

Let me tell you about it.

I went to the bus terminal with Jacob, in the colored door. The man at the ticket window must have been thinking about something else. After I paid him, he passed only a single ticket to Dalton through the hole and not a ticket back. "Next," he said. But I didn't leave my spot. I reminded him politely what I had paid and asked for the return ticket, and he apologized and pushed it through to Jacob.

Jacob doesn't own a fishing pole, but I had packed Hershel's old lunch-box with Hershel's tackle from when he was a boy in Dalton. It was settled neatly inside with socks in between. I told Jacob to be careful and not eat the baits and flies.

He looked at the red lunch-box and laughed. "Weeza!"

He had a brown suitcase, too.

"Uncle Frank and Aunt Olivia will meet you at the bus station," I told him when we took our places on the platform, "so don't be afraid."

"I'm not afraid," Jacob said. "I'm not afraid of anything. Poppa will be with me."

"That's right, as soon as he gets off night work." I saw the time on the waiting room clock, and I remembered thinking that since I had money only for Jacob's ticket, Hershel still needed to buy his. But I wasn't worried. Hershel wouldn't be late for this. I kissed Jacob twice while we waited on the platform.

Jacob calls Hershel Poppa, but Hershel is not his poppa. Jacob is my little brother, not our son.

Hershel has a big family. His mother Ruth and stepdaddy Ellis live with us in Atlanta. His brother Frank is married to a nice girl named Olivia, and they live outside Dalton with Olivia's family, including her mother and father and her younger sister Cora, who is fifteen.

I have only my Jacob.

I am Louisa.

Weeza.

Then Hershel hurried onto the platform, shaking

his head and waving his ticket. "Just in time," he said. "They made me do extra."

"We weren't worried," I said to him.

"Naw," Jacob said. "We weren't worried."

I kissed Jacob once more before he went up the steps onto the bus with Hershel. I watched him go to the back and find a seat near the last open window. Hershel sat on the inside of him. Then the white passengers got on, then the driver.

"Goodbye, Jacob," I said up to him.

"Bye, Weeza." He waved. The window was open a crack at the top. There was a man in one of the front seats, and I could tell he looked at me from the window because I have a figure and I can't hide that. I knew Hershel saw him looking because he stared at the back of the man's head when he was looking at me. "Bye-bye," I said to Jacob. I blew a kiss to Hershel, too. Then the man looked back at Hershel, but Hershel looked only at me then.

The bus drove off. I watched until it was out of sight. Then I left the platform.

Jacob is nine years old and tall for his age, but he is still a boy to me. Hershel loves Jacob like I do. They grew up hard together, Hershel and his brother, Frank, and they don't always get along now. I know stories about their daddy hitting them, but Hershel won't say much about it.

Like Hershel and me, Frank and Olivia have no

children, but they did have one who died a baby. A boy. That's why Jacob is visiting them now that school is over, to be like a family with them. There are creeks in Dalton, and the country is cooler in the summer and open, and safer. Jacob has known only Atlanta, though he might remember a little of Mobile from when he was very young.

He has lived with Hershel and me now since Momma went to Ohio to be with my grandma when she got sick. Hershel said Jacob would stay with us until Momma returned. But Momma never left Ohio when Grandma died five years ago; she just stayed in Columbus. She says it's because up north she can work at the counter in a white store and not have so many problems.

Hershel and I were married not long after she left, and it has been fine having Jacob live with us like our own son. I don't talk to Momma as often as I should, and Hershel never does.

I love Jacob with all my heart and want him to have a good stay in the country, but I already miss him. He promised he would call every day from Dalton, and I know he will.

Frank and Olivia don't have a telephone, though there is one in a Negro clothing store, which they'll let Jacob use every afternoon. I'll wait anxiously for his call just before supper, except for Sunday when the store is closed.

What else? Well, we have been to Dalton a few times over the years, all of us together, but not since the car has stopped running. I laugh sometimes when Hershel's stepdaddy Ellis tries to fix it (heal it, he says). He's no good with that car, but he tries. But since we walk to our jobs and the open market is near and Ruth is picked up by Mrs., we don't need a car much anyway.

I just miss my little Jacob and wish he was home again.

Monday, June 15

SIX

Bobby

When Monday came, their mother promised they would get going early, but the whole first day turned out wrong. She had said they would drive out of the city right after morning traffic, but they didn't end up leaving until afternoon, and even then it was late afternoon. Why had they waited? There was another phone call from his father midday; was that it?

The car had mostly been packed the night before and the rest was done in the morning by his mother and grandmother, but hour after hour it just sat in the driveway getting hot. Bobby had eaten four times already, waiting to get on the road.

Finally about three in the afternoon there was the sound of something breaking in the kitchen. "We'll start tomorrow," his mother said sharply, and something in Bobby's chest fell. Ricky threw his suitcase on his bed, growling like a dog. Then, just as they got used to the idea and Ricky grabbed the tennis ball and headed for the back door, the phone rang again and, not answering it, their mother stormed from room to room, getting everyone into the car.

What had just happened? There was no answer except the jumbled scene of the four of them piling out of the house and into the car, Ricky hooting softly to himself as his mother slammed and locked and relocked the front door.

The car roared to life. Under the sound of the grinding engine they were all quiet as they drove down Green, then Cedar, past houses and churches and parks and more houses and endless streets in the neighborhoods south of their house, then on Northfield Road into Shaker Heights and Maple Heights, past Southgate Shopping Center and Handel's Ice Cream, and Bedford Heights, then railroad tracks and factories and everything getting tangled in Northfield Center until all the streets slowed in end-of-the-day traffic and it seemed they would never get out of the giant city, and then they were out.

They were out, free of the close streets. Even at suppertime, summer was full-blown in the long valley you entered after you left Cleveland on the way to Akron. Green wet heat had settled over everything, and the white roadways had already thinned of cars now that school was over. The constant dipping and rising on soft tires made the big car seem like a boat as they sailed out of neighborhoods and past fields of dry grass alive with the late afternoon hiss of insects.

Soon they were traveling through small towns separated from one another by woods and plank-fenced and wire-fenced fields and overgrown meadows and old gray trucks, doorless and wheelless on blocks. It was new, all new, Bobby thought when the sharp smell of Queen Anne's lace came in through his window. It was pungent and sweet and full of summer, but cut sometimes by the faint smell of garbage or the closeness of exhaust fumes.

Early on, Ricky cranked his window all the way down, pushed a pillow to his cheek, leaned into the air, and breathed openly. The wind pushed his hair back.

Coming from Cleveland, Bobby knew what a city was. These were not cities. West Salem. Lodi. Many looked like villages that held no more than a few hundred people. The centers of town were all piled up to the roadside and ugly, except for a trim brick bank or post office, and, because they were making such good time, soon gone.

"I'm so hot," Bobby said, fanning himself with a

folded map, because the car still hadn't lost the heat it had built up all day.

"And one of us stinks," said Ricky. "Hint, hint, it's not me."

Bobby shifted his head to the right and pulled in a sour smell. He did the same to the other side which was not as bad. "It's the Hungarian in me," he said. "I sweat because of the Hungarian. I'm half—"

"Yeah, well, so am I," his brother said. "And I don't stink. You have to wear deodorant."

"It wouldn't matter if I did use it," said Bobby. "Mom said some people just normally perspire more. That's what sweating is. Mom said Hungarians—"

"Stop it!" said Grandma. "Stop it!" She turned around in her seat, her hawk nose silhouetted against the sunlight glaring against the windshield, her eyes moist and small. "Marion! Vhat are you telling them?"

Their mother shook her head quickly and kept her eyes on the road. "Bobby, keep quiet. Please. Or play a game. I want to make it past Columbus before we stop for the night." Bobby felt a slowing of the car, then a speeding up as his mother pressed down on the gas pedal. Was she mad at him again? He kept making mistakes. "You still stink," Ricky whispered. "This is the only way I can breathe," he said, and he pushed his face back into the wind.

Bobby knew it was hard to breathe with the wind blowing full in your nose, but Ricky kept doing it.

Shut up, he thought. Just shut up.

It was after that, thinking about his Hungarian blood and sweating and secretly sniffing his armpits again, and then watching the back of Grandma's head after she asked that they stop and she hurried into a restaurant to use the bathroom, that Bobby realized that Grandma's car wasn't even Grandma's car.

Why had it taken him so long to work that out? Two slow hours of getting used to sharing the back-seat with Ricky before he understood that Grandma's car wasn't even Grandma's car? *Grandpa* had bought the long green two-toned light-dark Chrysler for traveling the highways between Youngstown and Florida. *Grandpa* had bought it!

When the car door swung open and Grandma slid back in, Bobby now remembered seeing a snap-shot of his grandfather, his features tight, his eyes obscured behind glinting spectacles, standing next to this very car, its high fins, heavy chrome, and wide white sidewalls. It was made for traveling long distances on turnpikes, and Bobby had known this—or should have known—from the moment the car first appeared in their driveway, but the surprise of realizing it now made him speak out suddenly.

"Was this Grandpa's car?"

"Dummy," whispered Ricky as they pulled quickly onto the road again. "What's wrong with you?"

There was quiet for a while, then Grandma said, "Yes. It vas Puppa's car."

His mind was grinding so slowly. If it had been his grandfather's car, was it the same car stuck in the sand on the bridge?

Of course it was!

Grandpa had died because of this car!

Sitting forward on the seat, Bobby remembered the day his mother got the phone call. She said nearly nothing into the receiver, then put it down, not in the cradle, but on the table, the distant voice still speaking. Her face bunched up, her hand moving up to hide her eyes, she went to her bedroom and closed the door. It was the middle of the day. He and Ricky were quiet and stayed in their room. He heard her crying all afternoon and into the evening. His father went in and out of the room, closing the door each time. Bobby was afraid his mother was somehow changing herself inside that closed room, becoming a different person. Later, when she reappeared, her face was red and puffy, and she was quiet. He and Ricky had to stay at a relative's house while his mother flew to Florida and his father went back to school. ("What do you think, I can just leave my work?" "I don't know," she had said. "No, I can't do that. They don't care about that. It's the new semester. This is graduate school.") The man Bobby and Ricky had stayed with was a wide-faced, mustached Hungarian with wiry eyebrows who grew angry when Bobby did not eat fast enough. "Gerta!" he said, which wasn't a word Bobby had ever heard.

Leaning forward on the edge of the seat as they drove past brown farmland, Bobby imagined the big car stuck in a sandbank on a new bridge. Maybe only a few cars were driving over the bridge. Maybe none. Maybe Grandpa was out there alone. No, he remembered. There was someone else. There was a man.

Was it the rear bumper that his grandfather had been gripping, trying to lift it, when his heart failed? Another question: Had he been facing the car or away from it? Had he hooked his hands under the chrome bumper? His grandfather was not a large man. He was short and thin. Were his slender handprints and finger marks, those fingers that held the gentle pencils of his drafting kit—the empty one he had given Bobby that smelled of powdered graphite—somehow still there, smudging the chrome?

Or had he taken up position on one side of the car, his back to the fender, lifting the wheel well with upturned palms, as the passerby who had stopped to help (a truck driver, Bobby had heard), sat behind the wheel and depressed the accelerator to try to dislodge the car from the sand?

He finally didn't know any more than this: the car he was sitting in right then was the car that had killed his grandfather.

SEVEN

Cora

Don't look at a white person the wrong way or any way.

Yesterday afternoon Jacob and I didn't go to the Negro store, since it was Sunday and the store is closed on Sundays. So after the rain Jacob went fishing with his uncle Frank, and Olivia and I went right to town from church.

A family was walking down our sidewalk, so Olivia crossed the street, trying to pull me along with her fingers. But the cars honked at her running in front of them, so I was scared and kept back. Because of my new shoes I did not step into the wet gutter. And this family comes on up, a man and his wife and two boys around Jacob's age. I nearly held my breath. I knew the man's eyes were on me, you always feel that. I wouldn't look up until he was past.

Finally I looked up. It wasn't the man anymore,

but it was his wife, and the look in her eyes! As if I'd
have anything to do with her fat old man! She wore
a pillbox hat of powder blue with white pleats around
it. A short blue buttoned jacket. I wouldn't say she
spat on the sidewalk near my shoes. I wouldn't say it
if anyone asked me about it. But she did. Her two
boys didn't notice.

Maybe we should move again. I don't want to
live my whole life in Dalton and be buried near the
train yard. Not when there are stores like Miller's in
downtown Chattanooga.

But I did have a good time in the choir loft with
Jacob yesterday morning, looking down on those
heads with red necks and all that perspiration running in the crisscross cracks. The bald men sweated!
Tamping their necks with wet hankies. I nudged
Jacob and he rolled his eyes and I knew right then I
liked him lots. I wonder now if the man who walked
by, looking me up and down, was sweating in one
of those pews. I don't remember seeing that pillbox
hat on any lady's head, but then I wasn't looking for
it, either. Those folks never knew what we whispered
up there. I tapped Jacob and told him that being in
the loft, Negroes were a little bit closer to God than
those fat men were.

Jacob? It was all he could do not to laugh out from
his nose when I told him that. Sunday was a good
day.

EIGHT

Bobby

Just before sunset and still not out of Ohio, they passed through the town of Mount Gilead. It sounded old, like Ricky's battleground names, from a far-gone century, and not at all like Cleveland, which was clearly a city of airplanes and electricity and freeways. To Bobby, Mount Gilead was like all the other dim, stifling places they had passed since leaving home and was soon to be forgotten, until Ricky sat up in his seat.

"Gilead," he said, reading the road sign. "Mount Gilead."

"So?" said Bobby. He had seen signs for it for miles. "What about it?"

Holding one of his books up to the window, Ricky flipped page after page until he pressed his hand flat across a large map whose main feature was a long heavy line wandering from east to west. Making a sound in his mouth, he pushed his glasses up on his forehead and held the book close, squinting at it, until he pressed his finger on the map.

"Mount Gilead," he breathed out.

Reaching over the front seat between his mother and grandmother, Ricky fumbled for the TripTik, brought it into the back, and laid it open alongside the map. He glanced past the front seat through the windshield and Bobby saw him start to smile.

"Mount Gilead," he said again. "And Cardington and Ashley. We're passing through them all."

"So?" Bobby repeated. "They're crummy and little."

"So?" Ricky said without turning. "I'll tell you what so. The Lincoln train passed through every one of these towns. The train that carried his body after he was assassinated."

"Vhat?" said Grandma.

Bobby had heard of the Lincoln train.

"Listen to this," Ricky said, "from Euclid Station in Cleveland—you remember, Mom"—she turned her head sideways and nodded—"down to Columbus and then to Springfield, Illinois. It went through all these towns, into and out of all the train stations without stopping. It rolled really slow. Sometimes no more than five miles an hour. It left Cleveland at midnight and came through here during the night. The train rode down the tracks through every single one of these towns. Mom, it came right here!"

He searched out the side window now. "Can we stop at the train station? Can you find the tracks? I have to see them—"

"Oh, Richie," said their grandmother. "It's getting late."

"Mom, can you stop the car?"

"We're on the road . . . we kind of have to keep going."

"Mom?" he pleaded.

She shook her head slowly, then raised a finger instinctively at a round yellow street sign marked with a black X and two Rs. "There . . ." she said, slowing slightly and tapping on the inside of the windshield. "That looks like the railroad coming up. Maybe it's not too far . . ."

"Switch seats," Ricky said, and had practically done it before Bobby knew what was happening, then stuck his whole head out the right window like a dog. "Turn, Mom. Turn here. Go slower. Oh, cool!" He held his glasses to his face.

They took a slow right turn off the route and crawled east from the town center for a block, then two blocks, then several, for what seemed miles, and their mother started making sounds under her breath, until there was another road sign, and she slowed.

Ricky gasped. "There they are! The tracks. I see them. Drive across." And she drove the car forward on the flat road, nearly stopping where the dark rails sliced it, then rolled over them without power, until horns started honking behind them and they had to speed up again. After they had driven over the twin bands of scraped iron, laid out north and south along endless dry fields and trees, as inevitable and straight as lines drawn by a pencil and ruler, and they had turned back to the main route and finally left Mount Gilead, Bobby glanced at the book on the seat next to him.

Light was fading now from his side, but he could make out below the map a photograph of the Lincoln funeral car, and he imagined the train crawling like a dying person down the tracks mile after mile through the long night until it reached its rest.

That was April, too, he remembered. Just like Fort Sumter.

Had people crowded the tracks the whole way, in towns like that one, even in the lonely stretches of land between one station and the next—for certainly the villages and towns were not built up as now, but must have had far fewer buildings, more plains, more farmland, more . . . nothing?

The people must have numbered in the thousands, tens of thousands, just ordinary folks, lining the tracks in the depths of the night. Bobby could imagine them coming out hours before, in ones and twos and more, families gathering—*No, no, Joey, you can sleep late tomorrow. No planting* (or woodchopping or praying or whatever boys did back then). *This is important*—and neighborhoods, communities trickling out, sleepily at first, then streaming through the streets like a flood, talking to begin with, hailing one another, recognizing this or that neighbor, surprised perhaps at seeing so-and-so there, then growing silent as they all approached the iron tracks, taking their places side by side, sound draining away from them as they slowly lit torches and candles in the long wait, their hearts full and heavy and hurt.

And when it came through!

But before it came through, before that, they would have heard its gradual rumbling beneath their feet. Bobby knew they felt it, the ground moaning before they caught sight of the dark engine. He knew that feeling from waiting for the Rapid Transit that brought them downtown, and he imagined how out of the quiet they heard the slow ticking, then rocking, then clattering of iron wheels on iron rails, the breathing rhythm coming down the line before any sight of it. The muffled silence of thousands in mourning, taking the sound of that train into themselves, crushing their hearts flat.

And then it came!

The black engine, moving soberly toward them

on tracks laid straight across the land with such horrible certainty, and they themselves shocked speechless, as if they had never thought of it before: that something so irrevocable and heavy and iron could tame this mess of rolling land and life and forest. The somber bunting draped on the sides of the one car (out of how many cars?) that bore and carried the weight of the dark casket. The heavy fabric moving slowly in the slow air on both sides of the train. The coming of the train in the night, the train passing, the leaving of the train, vanishing slowly into the night, changing the world entirely. The weight of the great man's passing in the wheeled iron coffin, the lost, best president.

And did chocolates watch with their families? Were they right there next to the white ones? Lincoln was about them, too, wasn't he? Bobby couldn't quite remember their story. Were chocolate boys and girls there, too, up late like white children? *Time to see him, honeybunch. Wake up now. Time to see him one last time.*

Bobby felt his heart sink and sink as the sun sank and sank, his insides drowning in sharp hot tears.

Certain it was not the same and could not be the same and was utterly different, yet Bobby knew that they now drove the gathering darkness of the Ohio roads in their very own—finned, chromed, and plushly carpeted—death car.

NINE

Cora

"This is important," I heard Olivia say from where I was in my room.

She was talking in the kitchen to Jacob as he finished his milk. "You and Cora must find Uncle Frank. I can't go there right now. He's at the market. Or was supposed to be, but I think Cora knows where he is."

I came into the kitchen then. "I think I do," I said.

"Will you do that for me?" Olivia said to Jacob and me together. "Will you bring Uncle Frank home? With whatever bags he might have?"

"Sure we will," Jacob said, looking at me, so I nodded at him.

"And don't laugh if he jokes with you," Olivia said.

"Okay," I said. I knew what she meant.

So we two left together. We were as quick as we could be, but it was some walk downtown past the tracks, and we had to pace it. Jacob told me about fishing Sunday afternoon and how since it was not going to rain anymore he and Uncle Frank were going to go to the creek every morning till the end of his stay here. He said it was good Uncle Frank wasn't working at the rug factory anymore so they could go to the creek early every day. I said yes that the fishing might be good, but it wasn't so good that Frank was not making rugs now, and he shouldn't forget to call Aunt Weeza. He said of course not, he always remembered to do that.

I worry about Jacob sometimes. He looks older than his years and he whistles at fancy cars that we see. Two of them so far on the Dixie Road, and I don't know who was driving them.

"You can't whistle like that," I told him the second time.

"Sure, I can," he said. "I just showed you I could. Poppa taught me. I'm even louder than he is, and better." And he whistled again.

"I know that," I said. "I mean you shouldn't whistle like that when you are not at home with us. It's okay when you're home with us."

"I don't understand," he said.

"I know you don't," I said. I told him just listen to me, I knew what I meant. He said okay and didn't whistle after that, at least not when he was with me.

My sister Olivia was right. Her husband Frank was at the tavern as she guessed he was. I know why. He just lost his job and his friends were there. Olivia probably thinks if Frank sees Jacob when he comes out of the tavern it will shame him. I'm not so sure, but that's why she wanted us to go together. And also for me not to walk alone. Being tall, Jacob helps like that. I do like him lots. He can be so funny. Frank came out snorting and laughing and had three bags with him. "I was on my way to church. Honest!" But he wasn't funny, and I hushed Jacob's laughing as we walked him home.

TEN

Bobby

S o death was all around him.
From the moment he glimpsed those rusty
iron rails weaving off into the trees, Bobby couldn't
turn his mind from the ghastly railroad hearse of the
assassinated president—how it wound its way from
state to state, station to station, every mile from Washington to his faraway home, on rails like those.

In school he had seen photographs his teacher
had tacked on the bulletin board, clippings from
newspapers, all part of the lesson on Ohio history,
because the Lincoln train had passed through Cleveland on its way to the burial in Illinois.

The terrible circumstances of the president's death!
The evening dresses, satin and ruffled, the black suits
unutterably stained, the unspeakable spatter on the
box's tufted velvet chairs. That so-familiar face so
distorted. And didn't she say there was a smell? By

the time he—it, the body—reached Cleveland, they said the odor was awful, even outside in the park, where crowds passed by the open casket. Not only that, after two weeks the dead president's features had twisted and turned purple. Why had his teacher told them this?

"The better to love our greatest president," she had said, pinching her lips together, the classroom utterly silent.

But sitting in the car now, speeding away from the weedy rails, it came to him in a flash of remembrance what his mother had told him once: that Grandpa's body had traveled by train, too. From Florida all the way back to Ohio, his coffin had weaved its own way to burial, station by station, town by town, in a reverse journey to the one they were traveling right now.

But really? A casket on a train?

A casket draped with black shrouds, crape, and bunting? It was beyond terrifying. Squirreling up in the seat and closing his eyes, Bobby realized he didn't want to be anywhere but his own room. No one had died there. But as much as he tried to think of his bed and the wall it faced, he thought only of the long box.

Where exactly had they put Grandpa's coffin?

In the aisle? Did passengers have to squeeze by it

on their way to their seats? Did they have to reposition the cloths they had disturbed on their way by?

Or did trains have body cars? Maybe in front of the caboose? Or was the box wedged, unthinkably, in some sort of general baggage car, with trunks and suitcases, cartons of oranges, racks of hanging trousers and jackets, caged pets? Did they allow people to ride in such baggage cars, too? Were there guards of some kind? Railroad employees? Was the coffin in the train car where the conductors went for a smoke? Did they play cards on the casket? Did bums crouch in there among the baggage? Immigrants? Negroes?

His mind flying now, Bobby recalled seeing newsreels of Indians from India hanging on the sides and roofs of railroad cars. It was how they traveled. Were people like that on his grandfather's death train? Did they cling to the windows of the carriage with stalky arms, jabbering at the white man's coffin within? Oh, Grandpa.

ELEVEN

Hershel

I have been on trains.
   You know what I'm talking about. There was one car set aside for colored people. It was called the Jim Crow car.

It was a hot noon on the day I'm remembering, and hotter in the car, with us jammed in like sardines. There were heaps of baggage at one end of the car, too, which made it more crowded. There wasn't a casket this time. I've sometimes seen a casket in with the bags. They put them in with us, thinking we don't mind.

I had to go to Mobile because Weeza wanted me to talk to her mother, who was living there. That was six years ago. There was nothing I wanted to say to her, her cold eyes always staring me down. She never thought much of me, but I went because Weeza asked me to. I ate my lunch on the train. Weeza had packed it for me in my lunch-box. Now, that day the colored car was right up behind the engine, so I had to shield my sandwich from the cinders flying in the windows. Try that sometime. Even so, eating lunch in that hot car, crammed tight, with cinders in my eyes, was the last good thing that happened that day.

Another time a man stole my jacket in the train station. I saw him slide it off the back of the bench when he went past. It was brand-new. It was hot in the colored room and I had hung it over the back of the bench when I went to the restroom one last time. When I came out I saw a man swipe it off the seat and run off outside. He was a white man but he was a bum and he had come into the colored side and taken my new jacket. A woman on the bench yelled at him but she didn't get up, she was old. I wanted to chase that man and pull my jacket off him and kick and hit him, but the train came and I couldn't miss it. Negroes didn't want to be in that town at nighttime. This was when Weeza and I were first married and little Jacob was sleeping in our room. When I got home without my jacket and told her, Weeza took my hands into her lap and pulled my head down on her breast and held it there while I cried. I was mad as a hornet or a bomb. I wanted to hurt someone, but she didn't let me go until the sun left the yard and we were in the dark room crying together. She told me I was right not to chase that bum. I do some things right and some things that don't seem it.

Tuesday, June 16

TWELVE

Bobby

They hadn't reached Columbus after all, but stopped to pass the first night at a motel called El Siesta in the town of Delaware, still deep in Ohio. Bobby hardly remembered the drab walls of the room when they got on the road early the next morning, but he couldn't shake the smell of mothballs and dusty crawl spaces like the one in the ceiling over his room at home.

The engine droned hour after hour the first full day, into the hilly country just before the border at Ripley, where the Ohio River wavered between Ohio and Kentucky.

"Ripley was a huge Underground Railroad stop," Ricky said, flinging his arm toward Bobby's window. "There's a house here where it stopped. They still have it. You can go inside it."

Trains stopping at houses. Bobby didn't ask. The

moment they neared the end of the bridge over the brown river, Ricky added, "And . . . we're *in* the South. Kentucky started as a border state, you know. See these yellow states." He pointed to a page from a book. "Then it went Confederate and got bloody. It's a slave state. They had slaves even when they were in the Union."

Trains. Slaves. Bobby felt heavy and breathless. He cranked down his window and tried to fill his lungs with air.

Soon they were heading down through horse farms toward Lexington for lunch and the promised first battlefield site in a town called Perryville he had never heard of, even from Ricky.

But that was still hours away. The engine ground on, and so did the relentless boredom of the highway, past columned homes and meadows dotted with horses as unmoving as if they were stuffed. So they played car games.

"Highvay Touring Games," his grandmother called them, reading from the TripTik, and she helped the boys start playing them when they got restless in the backseat and didn't want to sleep or read or stare aimlessly outside anymore. Later Bobby saw what the TripTik said about the games: "Keeps Children Quiet and Occupied (For a While)." He thought it was funny for a printed thing to put in a little joke like that—(For a While). "For a Vhile."

There was "Highvay Bingo," where the first one to see five of anything shouted "Bingo" and won. Five cows. Five barns. Five blue station vagons. Five bums. Five hearses. Another was "I Am Tinking . . ." where someone says he is thinking of an object and names the letter it begins with. The person who guesses it gets to think of the next object. That lasted until Ricky started using words he knew that Bobby didn't—"Gatling" (machine gun), "ordnance" (artillery), and the absurd "chevaux-de-frise" (barricades made of spiked logs), and Bobby started yelling at him.

"Okay, cut it out," their mother said. "We'll be stopping soon."

Finally there was the game Ricky and Bobby had invented together. It wasn't really a game, and it was private so their mother and grandmother never heard them playing it, and it didn't have a name, but if it did, it might have been called "What If."

The point of it was to describe a situation in which it was impossible not to do something disgusting to yourself.

"Okay," Bobby whispered after they left Lexington, and his grandmother had fallen asleep with her head resting on the passenger window, "okay, I have one. What if you're in a desert. You're in a desert, and you're there for a week and you're starving to death, you're nearly dead, and it's incredibly hot, and then you find a bottle of mustard. All you have to eat in the whole desert is mustard. There's nothing else. It's just desert. And it's a hundred and fifty degrees. Would you eat it?"

"Mustard?" said his brother.

"It'll burn out your throat. You know it will make you throw up, it's so hot out, and it'll burn a hole in your stomach, but you're empty and you're starving. Would you still eat it?"

Ricky frowned. "Yellow mustard? Regular yellow mustard? Like for hot dogs?"

Bobby couldn't keep from laughing. "No, spicy brown. Hot. Like fire—"

"Boys?" said their mother. "Bobby?"

He lowered his voice and leaned toward Ricky, who leaned away as if he smelled sour armpits again. "It burns your tongue and that . . . hing unner yur tonnnnn," he said, holding his tongue up to show what he meant.

Ricky shook his head. "Gross. I don't know."

"It's been a week. You have no water. Your stomach is empty. It burns. And your water ran out days ago—"

"Then you just die from starvation," Ricky said.

"But no, because then you find a bottle of brown mustard. It might keep you alive, but will burn big holes from your tongue all the way to your stomach."

"I don't know. I guess so."

"You'd throw your guts up, you know—"

Ricky laughed now with a flicker of bitterness in his voice. "Yeah, I would. All over you!"

"Aww, gust!" Bobby made the sound of throwing up.

Grandma woke up when he said that and looked back, so they stopped playing. Her hair was funny, thought Bobby. His mother was just driving and driving, eyes ahead now.

Perryville was twenty-five miles off the TripTik route, straight west on country roads. It was middle afternoon when they turned off, and the snaking bands of trees along the smaller roads were shady and full of the early, still quiet of summer. Ricky fidgeted with his books for the longest time before he finally let them go and perched forward in his seat, casting looks out every window until he spied the sign—PERRYVILLE BATTLEFIELD—and they turned left and entered the park.

The road to the information center was long and straight and rising, and its shoulders were paved with gravel. They parked and got out. The sunny hills (there were always hills on Civil War battlefields, Bobby knew from the brown photographs) rolled so easily up and down and away from the car, overlapping one another like silent green waves, it was hard to imagine these fields as places of death. Ricky charged immediately up the nearest hill to a paved circle around a stone wall. Inside the wall stood an obelisk memorializing the battle and the dead. Beyond that several old cannons stood poised on a ridge. All around, the standing rocks, the bending flow of trees, the isolated groves moving ever so slightly in the heat, the long wooden fences zigzagging at the edges of fields, all were muffled, peaceful, and somber.

"You can't believe it," Ricky said, the first one to speak. "Places like this, a hundred years ago, there used to be thousands of guys fighting, shooting, riding. It was a mass of yelling men. Plus there was a fog of smoke, even if it was a clear day, from all the rifle shots, and who knew where you were."

"Yeah," said Bobby.

Following Ricky's animated charge back down the hill and beyond it to another hill and another, Bobby paused when he glimpsed a white house in the far distance below the crest. It stood angled at the bottom of the downward slope, near a sliver of creek, amid a loose gathering of trees in full leaf. The house was as unmoving and serene, he thought, as if you might gaze at it for hours and see no change at all save the sun's slow crossing, until a face appeared in its doorway, a woman's face, her hands wiping a towel, and she called you in, gently and by name, for lunch.

It was true, thought Bobby, you *couldn't* believe it. You *couldn't* understand how such peace could turn so deadly.

"It was the bloodiest battle in Kentucky," he said, recalling from a bronze plaque near the obelisk what he thought Ricky might like to hear, "1862."

"Sure it was. Thousands died here. Four hundred and ten on a small patch of ground, somebody wrote." Was Ricky making that up? "Their bodies all stacked up and ready to be buried," he added.

Turning, Ricky looked at the trees soberly, the sun on his glasses. Bobby wondered if so much blood soaking into the dirt burned the grass or made it grow better, greener. He couldn't believe it had no effect either way. It was blood. He asked his brother.

Ricky shrugged, not taking his eyes from the trees. "I don't know, but guess what? After some battles, maybe not this one, there were thousands of dead horses everywhere. Big, huge carcasses that had been shot out from under their riders. They were no good, so they just left them rotting where they died."

As they made their way back, the two boys saw their mother and grandmother walking out of the information center toward the obelisk, followed by a brown woman with a handled bag.

"What did they do with all of them?" Bobby asked. "The horses?"

"And the soldiers," Ricky continued, "the dead

soldiers? They'd pile the bodies in pigpens, *inside* the pens, with the hogs outside. If they didn't, the hogs would eat the bodies. The Union cleaned up their dead but left the Confederates for days. People had to wear masks over their noses. Also birds, too, would peck at them, but they shot those out of the sky."

"Gust," said Bobby.

They walked one last field down to a line of fences, stunned by a quiet that was quieter the farther away you went from the road. There were only two other cars. In the middle of June, only three cars. No one went to Perryville, the bloodiest battle in Kentucky history. Bobby looked once more toward the white house, but couldn't see it now. Grandma was sitting in the front seat, her door open, her feet on the road. She looked tired. Was she thinking of Grandpa? Did she know what a battlefield was? Did she care?

"How we doing?" their mother asked when they got back to the car. "We should be leaving. Moving on. What do you think?"

Ricky said nothing at first. Then, "Yeah. This is good. A good one to start with. It's great. Thanks, Mom."

"More to come," she said.

As they drove down to the main road, Bobby's mind drifted back to how his father often took

Ricky downtown to Indians games, how there was a giveaway at the grocery store once and his mother brought back a book about old pistols for Ricky while he got a book about watches, how Ricky did this and Ricky did that, and sooner or later any good thing Bobby did was remembered to have been done by Ricky, the first, best son.

He cursed to himself and turned away to the window but had trouble not thinking more of the same. He tried to wash his mind clean and stare blankly at the miles and miles of no change. Trees and white highways. Highways and gas stations. Barns, always barns, and rusting silos, and more highways.

Sometimes, tired of the ceaseless monotony of staring out, Bobby lay sideways with his back on the seat and his knees folded above him. He gazed quietly at the ceiling of the car while Ricky looked out the window from his pillow.

What did his brother see out there when he sat with his head against the pillow and his elbow on the padded door rest, cupping his chin in his hand? It wasn't the barns and horses and truck stops, he knew that. It was something farther away. Tomorrow, maybe, as silly as that sounded. Bobby didn't know, but it was far away. Ricky's face looked so small and pale and thin. He wrinkled his eyebrows when he thought people were looking at him, as if he thought that made him look better. He wasn't frowning now, so Bobby knew he was just himself, looking out the window at whatever it was. And whatever it was Ricky was seeing, it wasn't happy. Bobby knew it made him sad and took him far away from himself, but what was it?

Since the time he was five, Ricky had worn glasses and hated them. They were thick and heavy. Bobby remembered the first time his brother came home from the eye doctor with the glasses. Was their father there? He might have been, but he didn't drive, like Grandma didn't drive, so it must have been his mother who had taken him.

Embarrassed that the lenses were thick, but trying not to show it, Ricky boasted about them. He wrinkled his forehead and said that the glasses proved he was a genius. That girls liked glasses. That Clark Kent wore them. That he could see better with them than Bobby could without them. But the sight of his brother with those glasses broke Bobby's heart in a way he didn't understand. They made Ricky look thin, afraid, weaker than before, with only the frown on his forehead to defend him. How often, after putting the glasses on, Ricky would stare straight ahead and turn his face from side to side, watching the world ripple and distort across the lenses.

That was only the beginning. He had gotten thicker ones after that first pair. What was happening with his eyes?

Bobby tried looking through his brother's glasses once when Ricky was in the bathroom and had left them on the dresser. He was shocked at how blurry everything was. Their bedroom, the hallway outside their door, the whole world smeared with goo. What was it like looking through Ricky's eyes from the car window now? Had he really seen the railroad tracks as he'd told their mother? Had he not seen the white house at Perryville? Might he ever not see anything at all?

THIRTEEN

Grandma

The boys are two good boys.
They have whatever they want, they have
not been ever without anything, and their grandfather they didn't know well enough, but they are
two good boys. Their father? Nuh.

The older boy has eye problems, but so have we
all eye problems, except my Bobchicka, my Bobby.

Puppa had spectacles. They are on his face right
now in heaven. I put them on him before they took
him away.

I hope he will not go blind, my Richie. I hope
none of us will go blind. We have to eat well.

Their grandfather wore spectacles, but he was
sixty-six only. It was because he was an engineer,
always drawing, always bending close over paper.

August was a civil engineer and he designed

bridges, first in Hungary, then in Youngstown. He liked to visit new bridges and causeways and there were new ones built every few years over the water near Tampa and Clearwater.

I made chocolate chip cookies that day. I pulled them from the oven and slid the pan onto a cooling rack on the counter. I lifted one to look underneath, they were fine. I saw the clock, rinsed the warm chocolate from my hands.

August was as a young man a baker, with floury white hands the first time I saw him, but he loved my cookies.

The doorbell rang, and I knew it was Puppa. I answered the door, wiping my hands on my apron. "I've made your favorite—"

It was not him. A colored man stood on the doorstep. I locked the screen. There was a truck sitting at the end of the driveway. He wore big overalls. His face was still. He was colored and wore blue overalls and a cap that he took off and held in his large black hands.

"Mrs. Banyon . . ."

"Banyar," I told him. "What do you want?"

His lips moved. Sounds came from them. I cannot remember what he said but a few words.

". . . bridge . . . sand . . . hospital . . . tried calling . . . passed."

I threw the cookies away.

It was Puppa's house, too. He bought it for us. Like that, he was gone and never came home. It is empty now and will be also when I am there.

FOURTEEN

Bobby

The third day they crossed into Tennessee. It was happening so slowly. Bobby felt his stomach roll with every mile the car rolled. This many hours of driving was too many, and there were more than these to come—how many more, he didn't know—but the airplane ride stood fixed at the end of it like a beacon, scouring clean the time before it, so he said nothing. Maybe it was normal after so many hours of driving to feel sick from your stomach to your head, from just below your stomach to the hairs on the top of your head. He looked over. Ricky was staring out the window again.

Sometime late the night before, Bobby woke in the motel room to the sound of his mother talking softly on the phone. It was a quiet call, her voice no more than a murmur, but continuous, as if she were reading aloud. He almost didn't know when it ended because he hadn't heard her say any of the usual words, like "Good night" or "I'll talk to you tomorrow" or "I love you," just the gentle click of the receiver in the cradle. He cracked one eye open and saw her rise from the desk where the phone was, enter the bathroom, and close the door to brush her teeth. What had they spoken about? He heard the sound of the faucet and the swooshing of the brush soon after she closed the door behind her, which he took as a good sign. She was doing something regular right away after the call. Maybe it was an okay telephone call. Because wouldn't she be slow to brush her teeth if the phone call had upset her? She would linger, wouldn't she? She would look in the mirror at herself. Or just stand there. Or worse, she would cry. But not this time. His mother went right to brushing her teeth.

But the next day he doubted how sure he was that the phone call had ended all right. Not long after a short stop for snacks at noon his mother slammed her palms on the horn over and over, veered off the road, and skidded to a stop in the dusty shoulder.

"Marion!"

"Damn it, that's it!" she said.

The boys looked at each other as she turned off the engine with an angry flick of her wrist and stormed out of her seat, leaving the door open. She crossed in front of the car, stopped at the guardrail, and stared trembling into the trees. A truck roared by, then cars, one after another, then a space of no cars, then a long grinding ribbon of coming and passing and going.

"Holy cow," Bobby finally breathed.

"Marion," their grandmother called from her seat, and then said something in Hungarian. Whatever it was, she said it twice.

Their mother swung her head around. "So what?" she snapped, her whole body shaking. "I don't even care. He's mad. He's always mad. It wouldn't work, anyway, so what's the point?"

"But, Mar—"

"No!"

Bobby watched his mother step over the guardrail and off the side of the road, stumble a few steps, then collapse to her knees in the grass, and put her hands to her face and cry into them.

"What the heck happened?" asked Bobby softly.

"Dad, what else?" said Ricky. "On the phone last night."

"You heard that?"

"Vhat?" said Grandma.

What had his parents said, after all? Bobby tried to remember a word, any word, but couldn't, when Ricky opened his door and got out, passed behind the car, hopped over the rail, and went to his mother, standing next to her for a long time without saying anything. There was a tissue in his hand.

What had his mother asked, and what had his father answered? What "wouldn't work, anyway"? That word "work" sounded so ominous. What could it mean for something to not "work" between adults?

His mind flashed backward to the previous Christmas when his father hit him for making noise.

"You want to fight each other?" his father had said to the boys when their mother was working at her job downtown. They had been going at it with the fencing set Bobby had gotten for Christmas. The tree stood unlit in the front of the room, near the picture window. The fencing set's sword blades were plastic and rubber-tipped. Bobby had asked for them, but you can't fence alone, so Ricky had taken an épée and a plastic mask as "his own." Dancing in front of the tree, Ricky had struck Bobby's blade down, then lunged forward, snapping his own blade in half. Suddenly angry, Bobby punched Ricky in the shoulder and yelled, "That's mine, you stupid jerk!"

"Don't hit me, you jerk—"

His father came right out of the den, where he'd been working.

"You want to fight?" he said, his face red. "Yeah?

You want to fight? I'm working in there. I have two weeks. You want to fight? Okay, fight. But I'm going to take care of the first one who cries. So go on. Go on!"

Take care of the first one who cries. That was an odd thing to say, Bobby thought. But he and Ricky watched their father turn and leave and, seeing his broken sword on the floor, Bobby punched his brother again, and soon they were tussling, until Ricky kneed him under the ribs, Bobby sucked in a sudden breath, and exhaled with a cry. Ricky's eyes widened behind his glasses as he moved away.

Quick footsteps from their father's room.

Still on the floor, Bobby pretended his side hurt more than it did, holding his hand on it and wincing, but also setting his face firm and trying to look man enough to shrug it off.

It didn't help.

Through his grimace, he saw his father coming at him. ("Oh, crying, are you? Crying? Crying!") Bobby barely had time to scramble to his feet before his cheek was cupped in his father's left hand and his father came down fast with his right. The smack was loud and sudden, and he fell again. His cheek felt raw and red and shocked. Ricky watched from the couch as their father strode back into the den and slammed the door shut, opened it, and slammed it louder. Pulling himself to his feet, Bobby ran to his room and cried for an hour, muffled, into his pillow. When he heard his mother open the front door, returning to start dinner, he stopped. Telling her would only make his father madder than before. By that time Ricky was outside. Bobby joined him in throwing snowballs against the trunk of the oak tree until supper was ready.

"Stupid jerk," Bobby said.

Ricky shrugged. "Yeah, sorry."

"Yeah, sorry. I hate you—"

"Me?" Ricky said. "You hate *me*?"

This came back to Bobby in the minutes his brother stood by the guardrail, both of his hands empty now.

"We'll get to Chattanooga tomorrow," his mother said finally, rising and wiping her face with the tissue. Without her glasses, the brown circles under her eyes were nearly black. She spoke to no one in particular, didn't look at Ricky, raised her head as if trying to sniff away the last five minutes. "We'll find the battleground. I don't want to go now. I know it's close, but I'm tired. I don't feel good. I don't."

"Marion," their grandmother said.

"Shhhut . . ." his mother started, then her head suddenly flew around to his brother. "Ricky!"

"Yeah, Mom?" he said, startled by the sharpness of it.

"We'll spend most of the day at the battlefield, okay? I promise. At Lookout Mountain. Will that be enough for you?" She said this with a cold, crying look. "I said will that be enough for you?"

"Sure, yes," Ricky said, working his glasses back up his nose. "That's fine. Thanks, Mom. I'm sorry."

She waved Ricky back to the car and after a few minutes of breathing to calm herself got behind the wheel, saying nothing, and drove to the first motel with a vacancy sign and walked quickly into the office, leaving them in their seats.

FIFTEEN

Jacob

I know Weeza loves me. And Aunt Ruth and Uncle Ellis. And Poppa. And Olivia. Well, I'm lovable. I know lots of other things, too. I know I am a good speller in school. I know a girl in my classroom likes me, maybe two girls do. And probably Cora likes me, too. I know when Mrs. brings her car around to pick up Aunt Ruth—I am talking of Atlanta where I live, and Mrs. is the white lady Aunt Ruth cleans house for—I watch from the front window as she pulls the car up the street right to our house. It's brand-new and long, with fins the color of butter. Mrs. has to know I want to sit in it. She saw me staring at it from the window. Once I even came down the steps like she was driving up for me. I wonder if she would ever let me sit on those white seats.

The minute she saw me standing out there, Aunt

Ruth growled and shooed me back in the house to help Weeza wash up the breakfast plates. I ran!

But I didn't stop looking.

That car must ride pretty nice. I know I would drive it right out of here. *Kansas City here I come!*

Cora laughs behind her hand when I say funny things. She hides her teeth when she laughs. She says funny things, too, and almost made my nose explode in church with what she told me.

I get an idea sometimes. You know what I mean. I've lived in Atlanta my whole life, and that's a big city not a little town. I'm practically ten, or will be in a few months. And I'm tall for my age. Sometimes I think a thing and I'll say it. I've always been that way. I remember something about Poppa and my old momma. One day, he comes in and I say, "Poppa, why did Old Momma leave me here with Weeza and you and never come back?" And he blinks his eyes at me and says, "Never mind about that. You're with people who love you now."

Now.

He said "now." Like Momma didn't love me. Well, lots of people love me now.

Sure I know Poppa is not really my poppa. Once when I was supposed to be sleeping I saw him cry. Some white people did something to him. I've never cried but maybe once.

Being nearly ten I have seen a few things. I have friends down in Atlanta and they've seen things, too.

At three o'clock I'll go into town to an office in a store. Cora will walk down the sidewalk with me, but I know what to do. I just go left and left and right and left and into the store. Then I walk between the racks of clothes to the office behind the wall in the back and sit on the chair next to the desk. I know the number by heart, and I dial the telephone myself. There's a man there who's white. He probably has a car like Mrs. They all do.

SIXTEEN

Bobby

They stopped at a place called the Cumberland Motor Inn in a city called Wartburg. Funny name, he thought. Wartburg. Only it wasn't a city, but a small town that lay just off the highway in a valley surrounded by overlapping hills. The hills were covered with brown trees, but looked more like giant mounds of mud that rain had washed into peaks and creases that dried dusty brown.

The man at the front desk called a name and whistled sharply as his mother came out of the office, and a Negro girl with towels in her arms ran from somewhere to what Bobby suspected was going to be their room, but it wouldn't be ready for an hour, his mother said, so they ate lunch.

The cheery waitress at the restaurant up the street from the motel hovered over the table, first with water, then with her order pad, then with sodas, then with food, then just to see how things were going. They weren't going well. Bobby wasn't at all hungry, but his mother told him to eat, so he ordered the Sputnik Special from the children's menu. "Yes, little sir," the waitress said, which annoyed him. The Special was described as a "a meal to send any kid into orbit!" but was only a grilled cheese and coleslaw. Ricky ordered a sandwich and potato salad said to be "just like Mama used to make before television."

"Yes, sir!" said the waitress, smiling as she wrote on her pad, then leaving the table. Ricky chuckled. "They probably don't even *have* television in these mountains—"

"It doesn't matter," his mother said, sounding as if she was talking to herself. A blanket of quiet settled over them then, as if they were all too tired to speak. After the waitress slid the plates on the table and left once more, no one breathed a word. People at the other tables glanced at them when their own conversations faded. Bobby did not meet their eyes, but leaned over his plate.

In the motel room, his mother slept. So did he. The grilled cheese settled in his stomach like lead, and he felt it would sooner send him into the bathroom than into orbit. Gazing around before he set his head down, he realized he hated the room. It was too much like their room the night before in which he woke to hear his mother whispering on the phone. The cot's soft mattress smelled dully of someone else, a man, he thought, who smoked; but why would a grown man sleep on a cot? But this was the South. So who knew?

Finally, the room's heat fell over him, and he closed his eyes, trying to imagine the coming airplane ride but not getting far because he didn't know at all what it would be like.

When he woke, hours had passed, and he found he had a headache and no dreams to remember. His grandmother was sitting up in bed, praying with her eyes closed, while Ricky studied a large book of photographs by a crack of window light. Bobby looked out at the pool beyond. There were one or two people, a girl, a family, maybe, moving in the sunshine. It was afternoon and hotter than before. He turned over, rested his head on the mattress, breathed in shallowly, and slept again.

Later, he stepped out onto the little sidewalk between the room and the parking lot. It was nearly nine o'clock. The nighttime air was warm and scented with flowers and chlorine. His mother was still sleeping like she had the day she learned Grandpa had died. After the strange afternoon everything had slowed to a near stop, gone quiet, almost to sleep itself. They were far enough off the highway so that the air was hushed. Bobby felt that no one would ever find them there, if anyone was even looking for them. The mud hills twinkled with house lights far above the roof of the motel office.

He heard the sound of a faraway train whistle.

It came to him then what his mother had told him, that when there was a change of trains in Washington, Grandma had asked her to find out if Grandpa's coffin was being moved to the right train to continue its journey to Ohio. Had his father been there, too? It was Washington, where he was studying. But he wasn't part of this story, so perhaps not. His mother told Bobby she had been nervous, afraid, and dizzy. But after several wrong ones, she found the right counter and, clutching the stamped yellow tickets, asked a man at a window.

Bobby imagined a ruffle of papers behind the window, and a slow nodding: "Yes, ma'am. Your father's been transferred to track seven, leaving for Youngstown in twenty-eight minutes. I just made the call. He's safe."

Those strange words. "He's safe."

And his mother wobbling back to where Grandma stood alone in the waiting room, no more now than a stick of herself.

"He's safe," she repeated.

And Grandma's face, worn down to nothing. "Good."

He thought of uniformed men rolling the casket down the platform. Maybe they laughed. Certainly there was no way to disguise what they were doing among the holiday travelers. Was there a holiday? Maybe not. In any case, what they were pushing down the platform was undoubtedly a casket and it was going on a train and everyone saw it. Did Grandpa need a ticket like seat passengers? Maybe they didn't call it that, but it was still a ticket. He needed to reserve a place on the train. No. Two trains.

Across the parking lot, the chrome frames of vending machines sparkled under the bulb in the ceiling of the walkway. One was a bright red and white box the size of a refrigerator. There was movement at that machine. The girl he had seen earlier by the pool was bending over at the machine. Then she was up and turning around and facing him, holding something in her hand.

Candy? A soda?

Her hair hung to her shoulders. It was light brown.

"Huh . . ."

Bobby turned. Ricky had said that. He was standing on the sidewalk just behind him, the room door closed. How did he get there so quietly? He notched his glasses up his nose as he looked past Bobby at the girl, his brow crinkling to make him look older.

His sudden appearance reminded Bobby of the time he had spotted a quarter frozen in the sidewalk on his way home from school. He had exclaimed at it, then was amazed when an older boy pushed him out of the way, kicked the quarter free of the ice with the heel of his boot, and went off with it. He remembered how he told Ricky, who said he deserved to lose the quarter because he had said anything about it in the first place. Or maybe he only imagined Ricky would say that, but he had never actually mentioned the quarter to him.

"I remember her from the restaurant."

"The pool," Bobby said.

Ricky hooked one thumb in his pants pocket and shifted his feet.

Could a year make such a difference? What was Ricky thinking about the girl? Bobby thought about the girl. Of course he did. He had thought about her from the moment he had seen her at the pool, only he didn't know her hair was that long because she had worn a bathing cap to match her suit. Still, Ricky was taller, a year older, knew things about girls, and his thoughts were different and meant more.

"Let's get some ice," Ricky said, stepping in front of him.

"What for?"

"To get some ice."

They walked across the parking lot to the machines. The girl stayed there, holding a soda bottle in one hand while unwrapping a candy bar with her teeth. She took a bite, looking at Ricky.

"My parents drove me here because we're going to a horse farm to buy me a horse," she said, chewing.

"That must be fun," Ricky said. "What kind of horse?"

"Doesn't matter. I have two horses already," she said. "But one's getting old. I ride all the time."

"I've ridden a few times," said Ricky.

"You have not!" Bobby said.

"Shut up," said Ricky. "We're here to see the battlefields."

"You talk funny," the girl said. "You from up north?"

"Ohio," said Ricky.

"That's far away from here," she said. "I'm from Atlanta. My daddy works for Coca-Cola." She tapped one of the vending machines and laughed.

"What?" said Ricky.

"Coke bottles," she said. "You know. Glasses?"

"Oh, no," he said. "I always drink from the bottle."

"We'll see Chattanooga," said Bobby. "Lookout Mountain. That's where we're going tomorrow morning. Lots of guys died up there. Union and Confederate. Both sides."

"Oh," she said, tearing a strip of wrapper idly from her candy bar. She didn't say any more, except another "Oh." Then she walked back along the sidewalk to her room, trailing the scent of chocolate behind her.

SEVENTEEN

Y ou like her?" Bobby asked.
       "Maybe."

"You don't?"

"Maybe. What difference does it make to you?"

They were back in the room, whispering in the semidarkness. Grandma was asleep on the cot. Their mother was in the bathroom, its door cracked open, and a sliver of light shone vertically across the beds.

"Quiet now, boys," she said through the door. The edge was no longer in her voice. "Go to sleep. I want to get on the road early tomorrow. We can visit Chickamauga, then be up at Lookout Mountain before lunch."

Bobby turned on the couch to face his brother's bed.

"So what if you were rolled up in a rug?" he whispered.

"What?" Ricky said. Bobby couldn't see his face in the dark. "A rug? Rolled up in a rug? What are you talking about?"

"You know what I'm talking about," Bobby said. "With her."

"Boys," from the bathroom.

Bobby leaned closer to the shadow of his brother. "And it was a hundred and fifty degrees inside the rug and you and that girl were really jammed together but you couldn't breathe and she had bad breath and you had to go to the bathroom, what if you had to let it all go, both ways, and it would go all over you?"

"What?"

Bobby was laughing now. "It was all over both of you and it smelled and she had to go, too—"

"Shut up," Ricky said. Bobby knew he was stone-faced in the dark, while he himself kept laughing, breathless and unable to stop.

"And you threw up, too, blahhh, all over her face—" His heart pounded in his chest. "All over her—"

"Boys, hush up. Go to sleep!"

The crack of light grew bigger, and he could see Ricky's face now, glassless, his eyes staring at him.

"That's what you'd do to her, no matter what she was wearing, even if she took off her bathing suit—"

"You're a jerk. That's all you ever think about. Shut up."

"Even if she had on nothing at all—"

"Bobby!"

Ricky sat up in the dim light, pushed his glasses onto his nose, tilted his head both ways. After their mother left the bathroom, he got up and closed himself in it. Bobby felt a pain in the pit of his stomach and thought about the girl under the metal awning over the driveway, and his heart pounded and pounded. He knew the girl had meant that Ricky's glasses were as thick as Coke bottles.

EIGHTEEN

Frank

So, this is the time when I'm supposed to tell you things about me? I don't like talking about myself.

But I will say this. My brother Hershel never knew the worst of it.

It's bad having a father who knocks you around, which is why I say I may lose a job but I'm no drunk and that's not the reason. He was a mean man, angry at everything. I would never hit my kids like he did. Never raise a hand to them. Never could. Besides, Jacob is a fine boy. He can fish, even in the dinky creeks we walk to!

Truthfully, I think he is more like me in some ways than he is like Hershel. Sometimes I have to talk to him, to tell him what's what. But I never hit him. But he would get a pounding from Daddy like

I got. Hershel might learn it all someday, but I won't tell him. That's the past. There is such a thing as pride.

Nope. That's it. I have to go find a job.

NINETEEN

Bobby

W elcome to the Dynamo of Dixie."
      It was late morning the next day, a hundred and thirty miles south of the mountains. After driving around the wooded fields of Chickamauga, past stone markers and cannons and pyramids of cannonballs, and families at picnic tables, they were back up in Chattanooga, idling outside the entrance of Point Park and Lookout Mountain.

They hadn't been so far away, after all: only three hours from Wartburg.

Wearing a gray uniform and hat, a park guard sidled from inside the booth to their car. "You folks from up north?"

"Excuse me?" his mother said, pulling her arm into the car.

"From where in Ohio you from?" he said,

nodding forward at their hood, to mean he'd seen their license plate.

"No. Well, Cleveland. One of us from Florida," said their mother. "Cleveland, mostly."

"You far away from there now," he said, his eyes straying into the backseat at the boys before returning to their mother. Bobby remembered the girl at the motel saying the same thing. Then he noticed Grandma staring unblinking at the park attendant, staring him down, if he cared to see it, though he didn't look at her. Or was she simply trying to understand his accent?

"Different here for you," he said, oddly.

Their mother moved her head back. "Yes . . . what?"

"Just saying," he said, handing her a brochure, which Ricky snatched right away. "Parking's on the left at the top of the hill near the stone gateway. There'll be a place or two, if y'all look for them. Busy morning. Lookout Point closes at six for the evening."

"Thanks," said Ricky.

They drove around the upward-winding roads to the top of the hill, where they found an empty spot and parked. The morning was already heavy with the heat of the day to come. Grandma didn't want to walk much, she would stay near the car. She said something about not wanting to see "fields of death," because she had seen "Cossacks do tings" when she was young, whatever that meant. Her eyes had sunk deep into her face.

A few minutes later Bobby and Ricky were marching to the crest of the mountain. Ricky hurried ahead of him, on and off the paths, clutching at rocks and setting his feet among the scrubby growth so as not to fall. Heat dropped like a blanket over them.

"Lots died here, but we should really go to the Ridge," Ricky told him. "Missionary Ridge. That's the real place. Thousands died. But it's mostly houses now. Over there. And Orchard Knob, too."

Following his brother's gaze, Bobby looked over the basin of the city below to the crest of a long, wavering ridge on the far side. He sensed the battle there had been horrifying. Beyond horrifying.

Ricky had droned every mile from Wartburg to Chattanooga: how the Union general Thomas assaulted the Rebel troops on Missionary Ridge. It was a late afternoon charge up the defended hillside. It was reckless and unexpected, and it broke the Confederate line. The Rebels retreated to the town of Dalton over the border in Georgia, and the Union won Tennessee.

The idea of "late afternoon" was appalling to Bobby, as he gazed over the waves of heat toward the green ridge. There was a time, an actual hour, when a battle began? Even the word "battle" made it seem like a thing with a beginning and an end. It sounded like a unit of time and place. "The battle occurred in the late afternoon of the third day." But it wasn't like that, was it? It was all the hours before the fighting began, all the waiting for it, then the lifetime after the last shot was fired.

"Hey," Ricky said, falling suddenly to his knees in the dirt off the end of the path, his head down. Had he dropped his glasses?

Bobby decided that no battle in that dark war ever ended. He saw the distant ridge as if it were no longer green and hot, but blurry and brown like a wrinkled photograph, and heard the spattering gunfire that started late in the day—after *what*, hours and hours of troop movements over the land or hours and hours of dead time?—five, six slow shots over there, another closer, a crackling of tree bark, a pause when you thought that was it, then the air erupting in shouts and the *flack-flack-flack* of rifle shots all along the hillside, until their sound accumulated like the roar of some great engine.

"Get over here—" Ricky was burrowing amid a cluster of half-buried stones, digging at something in the ground. Bobby didn't want to talk to him. Turning instead, he spied a faraway tangle of trees between Lookout Point and the far ridge. Was that the place Ricky had called Orchard Knob or was it somewhere else? There was something obscene about the name. Knob? What kind of knob?

Closing his eyes, he could not avoid it. He saw old men and young boys hugging tree stumps to gain a moment's footing, that quick snap of gunfire, the scattering for cover, the stumbling and falling. And the gunfire! The more toylike it sounded—*pop, pop, pop*—the harder to reconcile the death it caused: those young boys that once fenced with sticks, played catch in side yards, snitched pies cooling on windowsills, or whatever they did, now spun completely around, their insides blown across the air.

Ricky was still rummaging on his knees. Their mother shielded her eyes with her hand, looking over at him. "Ricky? You should be on the path."

"Mom—" he said, his head still down.

Bobby imagined countless birds sweeping over a ridge now littered with boys whose stiff dead arms hailed no one at all.

"Look at this!" Ricky said finally. "Holy cow, look at this! Look!" His fist held up, he was bent farther to the ground, his face right down there in the dirt and digging at it with the fingers of his other hand. Bobby walked over lazily and watched as Ricky opened his white fist. Sitting in his streaked palm was a small rusty object, a metal slug, grimy, scratched, ridged, and looking old.

"A minié ball. A bullet from the battle. I found one!" Ricky said. He stood up, barely able to contain himself with excitement, rolling the snub thing back and forth in his hand. "I looked for more, but there was only one. And I found it!"

Bobby remembered that frozen quarter. "Let me see," he said.

Ricky's face was full and crimson. "This is history right in my hand. What if the soldier it killed rotted away, and this minié ball is all that's left? And I found it!"

"Can I see it?"

"Nuh-uh." Ricky stepped back, clamping his hand shut. "You'll lose it. Just wait till I show Dad. He'll know what this means!" And he ran up the summit like one of those countless soldiers until, stopping suddenly, he called out, "P-tchew! Ptchew!" Aiming the bullet at his chest, he drew it toward him and clutched it there, then hurled himself, jerking his body backward from the impact, and fell onto the warm grass, crying, "Tell—my— father—!"

Disgusted, Bobby walked down the slope past his mother without speaking. In the car park Ricky was still gushing about his find, letting his mother hold the slug. She wondered aloud if they should tell someone at the information center, but Ricky shook his head and dug the bullet into his pocket. Bobby imagined that his mother remembered the surly guard at the entrance booth and decided it was all right not to say anything.

Just before they gathered themselves to leave the mountain, Grandma had to use the bathroom. The gift shop outside the stone gate was a long low room, nearly empty. He and Ricky scoured the wooden boxes and the various cubbies ranged on long tables. There were pencils with printing on them, yo-yos, harmonicas, jump ropes, marbles, maps, books. There were medals, cups, clothing, and wooden pistols and plastic sabers that reminded Bobby of his fencing set. Ricky's head swiveled everywhere, then he made a sound and ran for a table stacked with slouch hats that he had told everyone were called kepis. They were made of pressed felt—some blue, most gray—stiffened into shape. Ricky dropped one then another over his head and, removing his glasses, looked in the oval mirror provided in the center of the table, wrinkling his brow this way and that.

Bobby stayed at the tables of cubbies, where he found one piled with small cloth sacks with red words printed on the outside and knotted yellow draw-strings at the top. Bobby felt something hard and small inside a sack. He loosened the drawstring.

"I'm going out here," said their mother, catching the attention of both boys and pointing to the rest-rooms in the hallway outside the shop doors.

"Wait. Me, too," said Ricky. He trotted away from the hats to the men's room outside the shop.

Bobby turned the little sack upside down over his palm and a snub of lead fell out.

"Are you kidding?" he whispered.

It was a bullet, identical to the one Ricky had found below the slope, only it was shiny and new. The wooden cubby was full of them. They were not real slugs. They were souvenirs. Ricky must have discovered one of these, a fake bullet lost by a tourist—maybe a boy like himself—and had presumed it was a hundred years old, heavy with history, an artifact of the bloody battle.

Glancing behind him, Bobby saw no one watching. He returned the slug to the cloth bag and with his hands low on the table slipped it into his jeans pocket. It was only a dollar. Less. Sixty-five cents. No one would know.

His chest pattered as he moved away from the table.

"Bobby!"

He spun around. His grandmother was at the door. "Bobby. Come. Ve're leaving now."

Soon they were outside, heading for the car.

Bobby walked behind the rest of them. He slid the bag from his pocket, opened it, and dropped the slug on the grass near the pavement, and the bag a few feet away.

"Hey, look at this. Ricky. Look at this." He remembered they were the same words his brother had used on the battlefield. When he saw Ricky turn, he bent down and picked up the shiny bullet.

Ricky came over and looked in his hand. "What?" He put his fingers in his pocket to feel the slug he had found on the hill.

"There was a table of them right there in the store," Bobby said, rolling the bullet back and forth across his palm. "Didn't you see them in there? They look pretty real, don't they. But they're not. I guess you found one that somebody lost or dropped. See, here's the bag," he said, bending down to retrieve it. "It's just a souvenir."

Looking at Bobby's palm as if hypnotized by what he saw there, Ricky pushed his glasses up, but his head was lowered, and they slid down again. He wasn't getting it. "No . . ." he said. He pulled out his dirty bullet and compared it with the one in Bobby's hand.

They were the same.

"Yeah. It's a souvenir," said Bobby, looking at the two slugs. "Wash yours off, it'll be shiny, too. Sixty-five cents. Not worth anything." He was breathless now.

Then, almost softly, Ricky said, "You little jerk."

"What?" asked Bobby, trying on a little smile as

if he hadn't understood the meaning of his brother's words. "What do you mean?"

"You little jerk," Ricky said again as softly. His face was bunching up, his glasses slipping slowly down the bridge of his nose. Even in the abundant sunshine of the parking lot he looked pale, more so because of the bright reflections from the cars all around him. "You thief!" he said loudly now, his face still looking down at the hand that held his dirty bullet, his glasses nearly off the end of his nose. "You little thief—"

Then his hand fisted around his bullet.

Bobby stepped back. "What? You want to fight? You want to fight, huh, Coke-bottle glasses? Bottle glasses! Yeah?" He reached into his pocket, slid out the stick knife, and wiggled it in front of Ricky. "Shut up! Shut up! Jerk! It's fake! It's damn junk. Your stupid Civil War. Blindy—"

He didn't hear the sound of the twisting gravel behind him, but his mother was suddenly there, wheeling his shoulders around and smacking him sharply across his open face. "Give me that! Give me that!"

Bobby's cheek stung as if it were scraped with a file. He pulled the knife away from her, as Ricky had pulled the bullet away from him. "Give me that!" she screamed. Bobby threw the stolen bullet and its bag angrily at the ground and ran off into the trees beyond the parking lot.

"Bobby! Bobby!" his mother called, but he didn't stop.

"I hate you all!" he shouted over his shoulder. He felt like a trapped animal and ran as if his cage door had suddenly swung open. When he got to the trees, he slowed and turned. He saw his mother's hand bunched around something as she helped Grandma into the car. Her face was tight, spitting mad. Was she crying? Were they both crying? Ricky was staring at the ground nearby, looking lost. Was he crying, too? Bobby's chest stung from shoulder to shoulder, as if poisoned. It was all stupid little words: "Jerk!" "Shut up!" "Give me that!" "I hate you all."

But he didn't hate them all, did he? He hated something else. Being in the car for days. Being in the bewildering South. Being surrounded by death, everywhere death. Being himself. He felt ashamed, but he didn't know why. Ricky was a jerk. He *was* a jerk. That girl in the rug with nothing on. But there was something else he couldn't name.

Looking up the hill, Bobby couldn't stop it coming, the fall of bodies at him and on him. He felt them falling off the hill directly at him, moving through his stinging chest and out his back, taking his breath away, taking little bits of him when they fell. They came on like the whistle of a coming train, the piercing shrill call. The coming of the train in the night, the train passing, the departure of the train, its slow vanishing into the night, leaving him utterly empty of everything but pain.

I'm sick, he thought to himself, his cheeks hot and dripping. I'm sick and I hate all of this! It was all he could think of, there were no other words, but he knew they weren't right, they weren't all of it, but he could find nothing else except to run growling away into the dark trees.

With garbled curses, no more than animal breaths, he gripped his wooden knife and jabbed it hard into the ground, carving a circle of dirt deeply into it. He pried it up and out, a cone of moist clay tipping over onto the ground, a fresh blossom of earth. Looking down the slope over the car park, he saw his mother marching Ricky tenderly back to the store, her arm cradled around his shoulders, his head bent low. She clutched the stolen bullet in her other hand as if it were a bomb, its fuse the dangling yellow drawstring. Bobby's eyes fixed on the ground between his knees, and he snapped the knife in half and in half again and dropped the pieces into the hole. Then he replaced the clod of dirt and stamped it down flat, stamped it, stamped it, then he stumbled slowly to the car where his grandmother sat not sleeping but wordless, staring away, with her tilted head against the window.

TWENTY

Jacob

The sun is going down behind the trees, but the air is still warm like a blanket over your face. That's okay. It's still cooler than Atlanta. It's the water always moving in the creeks and the wind in the trees and not so much pavement that makes it cooler.

A person needs time on his own sometimes. It was just too small and hot in that kitchen, the two of them singing and cooking, Cora and Aunt Irene. So I left them jibber-jabbering at the counter, and see where I am. Fishing was all right today but too short, since Frank had to look for a job, and I want to sit on the bank some more. See, I have his best pole and my box of baits.

The road is getting long shadows across it now the sun is leaving. Some birds singing. Fewer now than before. Is this the road I walked with Uncle Frank and Aunt Olivia that first day after we left Hershel at the station? It should be the same, but it doesn't look the same now. Maybe that's because of the sun going down behind the trees and shade coloring the road. Or maybe there was a road I forgot to turn on.

I don't know why Uncle Frank got so mad at me that way. Everyone is always getting mad at me.

"You shut up and you stop that," he said. His eyes were small like buttons. "You just stop that!" He yelled it.

No. I do remember. It was because of something I said about Mrs. and her red lips and her yellow car. That I would drive it someday soon and she would let me. Was that all I said? I say too much. Never mind. It's only Dalton and I'm from Atlanta. Cora says things to me all the time. No one heard me anyway except some tangle of people at the market counter. I didn't say anything bad, did I?

A little farther to the creek. I think I'll sing to keep myself company. Frank is funny sometimes. Like when Cora and I brought him home from the tavern. The "market." That was funny. It wasn't any market.

The road curves up ahead. That's not right. It's nearly been an hour. I should be there already. Maybe more than an hour. Maybe it's too late to fish the creek now. I didn't say anything bad, did I? Who heard me if I did?

Gonna be standing on a corner,
Twelfth Street and Vine.

I talked to Weeza only twice because she wasn't around yesterday when I called. It was early. I just want to be home with her and Poppa now. I don't want to fish here anymore. I better go on back. Is this the way? It still doesn't look right. Maybe that turn ahead.

Gonna be standing on a corner—

Something's making noise in the shadows up there. Someone running now?

TWENTY-ONE

Bobby

"Are ve lost?"

Ricky flicked his eyes up at Grandma and said, "I don't know."

"Nuh. Ve are lost."

"I don't know," Ricky said.

They'd left Chattanooga in the early afternoon, Bobby gazing sullenly at signs that said Ringgold (there was another battle there, but they didn't stop) and Tunnel Hill and Dalton, and after another drive-through at Kennesaw Mountain National Battlefield Park, had reached the outer streets of Atlanta before supper.

Atlanta was a huge city, flat, ugly, and sprawling away from the route they were on.

Ricky sat between their mother and grandmother in the front seat, commanding the maps. Though shadows were already growing over the streets, and they were beyond tired, there was one more site to see before they stopped for the night.

"It's in the guidebook," their mother said, hunkering over the wheel. "I read it before. The big house is right out here somewhere, and the memorial for the Union soldiers."

The tension in the car was electric and silent and heavy. Every breath Bobby took was wrong. He was a criminal now. A thief with a mean streak, an animal, while his brother was sainted.

"I don't know, Mom," Ricky said, blinking through the window and removing the blue slouch cap his mother had bought him at the gift store when she returned the stolen bullet. "Why would they even have a Union headquarters in Atlanta? Georgia is a Rebel state. Why would they keep it as a place to see? They hate the Union. They hate Sherman because he set fire to Atlanta. And why would there be anything down such a junky street, anyway? Practically right on the railroad tracks."

She pressed forward. "Because the guidebook says so. It's in the Triple-A. The Union cemetery and the headquarters. And it's this way."

The car edged along the narrowing road, which buildings pressed even narrower. There were low brick and cinder-block structures and high-windowed warehouses. Tiny sheds and dismal, large-doored depots.

"Well, it doesn't make sense," Ricky said. He held the map up to his face and scanned the lines on it. "This map stinks."

"Ve are lost. Nuh."

"We are not lost. We're not lost. I'll just go down here," their mother said, barely slowing into a turn, "and if it doesn't work . . ."

"Marion," said her mother, "vatch out, the fence—"

The right headlamp nicked a length of fence that was bent in toward the road. Bobby pulled his face back from the window. There was a squeal and a crack.

"Marion!"

Bobby looked at the back of his mother's head. She made a sound on her tongue and slowed. "All right—"

"We don't have to go here, Mom," Ricky said.

"I'm here," she said. "I'm already here!"

Farther down, the road wound even closer between buildings on one side and a link fence on the other and led directly toward the crisscrossing tracks.

"How do we get out of here?" asked Bobby.

No one answered. Of course not. Why talk to him? His mother hunched over the wheel, looking out the windshield to the left. What was she looking for? Had they gone down the wrong road? Maybe they'd made a bad turn off the main street. What was wrong with the maps? Had the street sign been twisted? Bobby remembered that maybe it had been. Maybe it was pointing the other way and they'd made a mistake. Maybe it was done to trap people. Isn't everyone down here against you anyway?

"It looks wrong," Bobby whispered, half to himself. He searched out his side of the car, then the back window, then the other side, knowing his words sounded odd after so long a silence, but hoping this mix-up might allow him a way to start talking to them again.

Then the pavement stopped, and the road was packed dirt and narrower still. Maybe it wasn't even a road. There was no place to turn around. The way ended near a couple of low wooden buildings that might be storage houses. A car was parked next to one of them.

Dust flew up when they passed a warehouse leaning at the road, and then, in the gap between the buildings, standing up on a hill behind them, they saw a dead house in a field of high grass.

TWENTY-TWO

James

W hat do you see?"
  "Nothing."
"Nothing? Then what are you looking at?"
"Car."
Jimmy's brow was wrinkled at what he saw going on out the window. One suspender dangled loose below his belt. He held his tie in his hand. I knew he had to leave.

"Who'd think anybody would come here and block up our road?" he asked. "I have my job to get to."

"So go out and help them," I said.

"Who would come here?" Jimmy said.

"Northerners," I told him, pushing my chair away from the table and smelling now the steam iron from the other room. "Coming to see their Yankee house up the hill. You know that."

"They'll hit my can," he said, leaning both hands on the sill.

"I'll hit it," said a sweet voice from the other room.

"My *ash* can," Jimmy said over his shoulder.

"I'll hit that, too!" said the voice.

"Aw, honey." Jimmy shook his head, then looked more closely out the window. "Driving all over creation to see their Yankee houses."

"So go out and help them," I said. "Or I'll go."

"We can't go out there, Dad," he said. "They'll say we robbed them."

"Yeah, and you got dressed up for it, too," I said, pulling the back of his shirt down from where it bunched under the suspenders. "Look, Ohio plates. Told you. They're just lost."

"Lost? Then why's she driving so fast?"

I laughed. "To see the Yankee house!"

"Can't they see it's a ruin?" Jimmy said, flapping his tie around his collar. "Atlanta wants to forget that war ever happened."

"Lincoln happened," I said to him, feeling clever for having thought of it. I liked the way it sounded.

"Aw, Dad," he said.

"Lincoln happened," I said again. "And just see how good off we are!" I waved my arms around the room and laughed and heard Jimmy's wife chuckle from behind the door. With that, I was done and sat down.

Jimmy grunted to himself, watching from the open doorway now, and said over his shoulder without looking away from the dust coming up the road, "Lincoln died of a hole in his head and that war never happened and she's going to hit that can!"

TWENTY-THREE

Bobby

The dead house was surrounded by wild trees. The bottom-floor windows were boarded up, the upper windows shattered open. Paint on one whole side of the house was worn to the wood. A couple of smaller buildings nearby were leaning and roofless. The grass in front of them, growing up the hill from the roadside, was two feet tall. There were a few rounded, tilted heads of grave markers lost in the weeds. The air smelled of tar and pine needles and coal smoke.

"That's it?" said Ricky, holding open the guidebook, almost snorting disgust like his father. "That's the Union headquarters? That's the cemetery for the Union soldiers? It looks haunted."

"Maybe it is," said Bobby, his first words to Ricky since the bullet on Lookout Mountain.

"Look how they ruined it," Ricky said, but not to him. "They hate the North here. Nobody likes us. Did you notice that?" He said this to their mother, almost angrily, like their father might have. "Look what they did to the place."

"Who?" said Bobby. "The chocolates?"

"Bobby!" said his mother. "You are really asking for it."

Ricky made a noise in his throat. "Not them. The regulars. They hate us. Negroes don't hate us. We freed the slaves."

Negroes. His brother said Negroes.

"We did?" asked Bobby.

The squeak of an opening door hinge behind them. Bobby turned. The door on the building near the road was swung wide. A black man was coming out. He wore a white shirt and a tie.

"Oh, my God," his mother said, looking at the outline of the man in the doorway. "Get back in the car."

"Ma'am . . ."

"Just get in—"

They climbed back into the car, and she started up, shifted into reverse, and gunned the engine. The tires spun in the cinders, scattering them against the undercarriage of the car. When the tires grabbed finally, the car jerked back into the garbage can at the bottom of the steps, knocking it over, crushing it, and flattening two fence posts that held up no fence. "Oh, my God—"

"Puppa's car!" Grandma said.

A louder voice from the house. "Hey . . ."

Electricity shot through Bobby. "Mom—"

"Marion!" said his grandmother.

"Quiet, both of you!" said his mother.

Grandma's mouth dropped open as if to say something, but nothing came out. Her eyes were fixed on the black man. She crossed herself. She said something under her breath, biting her lip.

Two men were coming toward the car now. The one in the white shirt was younger. The older one wore gray pants. Were they angry at them for crumpling their ash can? Bobby's hand reached for the window crank, jammed it around until the window was closed, then held it fast. The men came down two steps toward the car, and Bobby and his brother shared a frantic look.

"Mom—" said Bobby. "They're getting closer—"

"I know! I know!"

The right front of the car slipped off the road and into a fence. A loud pop.

"Oh, my God!" said their mother, the car moving forward only slightly, swaying, but she didn't release her pressure on the gas pedal. "The tire—"

The men's faces were clearly visible now. Bobby

saw eyebrows crinkling, eyes squinting. One said something he couldn't hear over the noise inside the car. The older man raised his hand at them and said something else. His palm was light, almost pink. Bobby's mother tried furiously to get the car back onto the road, jamming her foot down, moving the wheel back and forth, cursing, pumping the pedal, trying to escape before the men came too near. He imagined how absurd they must all appear, the crazy scrambling inside the car, while outside the Negroes were able to just walk up to it. The car did not move forward, but slid sideways, spitting up cinders behind it, as if stuck on something. Were they hooked into the fence?

"This is ridiculous!" his mother said. "Totally ridiculous!"

Bobby remembered with horror the sandbank on the bridge and wondered if the car was cursed to get stuck in things. What if they'd have to get out to dislodge it? The engine whined and the wheels spun as the men approached his window, motioning to the back of the car. The old one's face was heavy with folds. His lips were strangely wet and alive and moving, but the car noise was too loud to hear what he was saying. His eyes were pinched nearly closed because of the dust.

"Mom—" Bobby said. "Maybe he just wants—"

"Keep quiet!" she shouted. "My God, keep quiet!"

The younger man was right up at the car now. Then he shouted something and started kicking at it. Bobby's mother screamed, hit the gas, and cranked the wheel one more time. The car lurched forward out of the ditch, taking a section of fence with it, bounced onto level road, then coughed and stalled. Their mother forced the stick on the steering column to the left. "Oh, my God—"

"Mom, maybe he was unsticking us—"

"Bobby, shut up!"

The older man was there again, still speaking. He reached his hand to the window at Bobby's face, his pink palm moving at him. The car raced suddenly and the man with the tie jumped back with a shout. Did he swear at them? The other tried to knock on the window.

A sharp gasp. "Oh . . . Marion!"

His mother cursed, then revved the engine loudly and tore off, leaving the older man with his hand raised to his face, the other still yelling out indecipherable words. The engine raced as if it would whine off into space, and they stuttered down the road on one burst tire, dragging a length of metal fence. Bobby looked out the back window. A figure was moving in the open doorway of the house now. He saw a flowered dress. And a silver glimmer. An iron? There was a woman in that tiny house? *A woman?* She turned away from the car and was back in the shadow, while the two black-faced men, voiceless, stood next to each other, staring, arms moving up and down. Were they waving away the dust or calling out to them?

The Chrysler twisted swiftly along the narrow road, finally giving up the fence it had dragged hundreds of feet, but nicking the walls of buildings over and over, until it bounced out on the main street, flopping on its one airless tire, toward a truck turning from the other lane.

Ricky yelled, but their mother had been going too fast to safely turn the wheel. She jerked it once and slammed the brakes hard, so the car struck the curb full on. A second tire burst, and the car lurched up hard into a chain-link fence and a telephone pole, cracking it—the pole fell across the fender, and steam exploded from the buckled hood. For seconds everything stopped.

"Who's hurt?" said their mother. "Is everyone okay? Mom?"

"I'm not hurt," Ricky said. Grandma's forehead had struck the dashboard, but lightly. It was dull red, not bloody. The truck had already gone down the street. A dented car with a black face at the wheel drove slowly past, its driver leering openly at Bobby, but not stopping.

Bobby released the window crank, his fingers strained and white.

"I'm okay," he said.

Friday, June 19

TWENTY-FOUR

Cora

I t was fiercely hot this morning. Of course I didn't sleep all last night. But as tired as I was, I was stark awake by the time I saw the tracks at Dalton center. Everything was silver in the heat coming between the buildings. I passed by the stand on the corner and pushed open the door of the store and went between the dress racks all the way down the corridor to the office where I knew that telephone was, and I stood there. When the man put down his pen, he raised his face and made a big smile as if nothing in the world was wrong.

"Hello there, Suzie. Early today. Where's little Jacob this fine morning?" he said.

I waved my hand in the air because I wasn't ready to say that. I told him that my name was not Suzie, that Hershel is the brother of my sister's husband, and I needed to call him in Atlanta. The man motioned his hand at the chair across the desk for me to sit down, and I did.

"I know it, dear. I know your name's not Suzie. I've seen you," he said.

I can't pretend to know what he was thinking, but he looked my face all over, then shifted in his seat and picked up the telephone. I am fifteen. He was large with brown and gray hair and stains on his shirt and had a face like a fat pink balloon, but he didn't dare say anything nasty, since the store manager, his employer, is a Negro known to my father, and it was them together who fixed it for Jacob to use the telephone. What made an old white man come work at a Negro store anyway? He smelled like a saloon, so I guess he was happy to have this job. Nobody else wanted him. If he was in church maybe he should be up with us. That's the kind of thing that I know would make Jacob laugh. Only when I thought of that I got scared.

The man pressed his big pink finger up and down on one of the two black buttons at the top of the telephone. He held the telephone to his ear. While he did, I breathed slowly, trying to remember what I was about to say and how to say it.

"Ya know," he said, "there are some say your people don't mind where they're at. We take care of the Nigra pretty well. No need for boycotts and sit-downs and such. Now, I ain't saying—"

I looked at my hands in my lap, and he stopped talking or I stopped listening and then he stopped talking. Momma taught me never to speak to a white man about that, that there was no good answer to it. And you never meet their eyes. He held the telephone for a little time at his big pink ear, then he handed it to me.

"Hello?" I said into it. "Hello, is that Hershel?"

"No, no. You have to dial the number, Miss," he said. "It's Miss Cora, isn't it?"

He knew that, he must have. I nodded. "Yes, sir. Cora Baker."

"Well, Miss Cora Baker, you have to dial his number," he said again. "Everybody got his own number. On that paper you got there. You ever done this before? Jacob done it twice hisself already. Where is little Jacob today?"

I looked at the scrap of paper Momma had given me. I didn't understand what the man wanted me to do.

He reached his palm to me. "Show me the numbers and I'll dial them, dear. I did it for Jacob this way before he did it for hisself twice already. I like the Nigra people, you know, like 'em lots. Then you listen. And someone will talk. Then you talk. No, just the paper, you keep the receiver. Now you hold it up to your ear. Yes, that's right. Wait a few seconds."

I held the telephone to my ear while he looked at the numbers on the paper and pushed his fingers around the dial on the telephone. He did it quickly. He does it all day long, I thought. At first nothing happened, then there was a faraway sound of clicking, then nothing, then clicking again. It was the first time I had heard a voice so far away say, "Hello?"

It was a man. "Hello?" he said. "Is this Jacob?"

"Hershel Thomas?" I said.

"No, he's my stepson. This is Ellis Vann, his stepfather. Who is this?"

"Please let me speak," I said, running the words over in my mind and trying to get through them and determined not to cry in front of this man.

"Shall I get Hershel on the line? *Hershel!*" the man said, sounding farther away.

"You will want to know this," I said, starting in as I had memorized it. "Your boy Jacob has been missing since yesterday evening—"

"What?" the man said. "Little Jacob? *Our* Jacob? *Hershel! Get in here!*"

"Jacob," I said, "is missing."

There was clicking on the phone, then the man said, "What?"

The man with the pink face, his mouth dropped open.

I said into the telephone, "We have tried, Olivia, your sister-in-law, has tried to find him, and your brother Frank, but they have had to go to the Dalton police and tell them he is missing."

"Is this Cora? Put Frank on the phone."

"But the police say he is a Negro boy and anyway has not been gone long enough to look for. Perhaps you will want to come here to Dalton to your sister-in-law Olivia's house."

"Cora!" he said. "You're saying Jacob isn't with you?"

It was strange to hear my name.

"Yes," I said. "This is Cora. Thank you."

That is what I said, and that was all I could say if I was not to cry. I handed the man back his telephone and got up and went down the corridor. Then I turned back and said, "Thank you," to him, and his mouth was still open. Then I walked back through the racks to the door and ran home. I knew his eyes were on me all the time I was in the store. You think I'm brown, you think I'm a Nigra? Well you're white and work in the back of a Negro store.

The way home was long. My shoes and feet were dusty when I walked up the steps into the house. For some reason I remembered that pillbox hat and the church and Jacob whistling and then us laughing at the fat white men together and again Jacob whistling at cars, and then I grew really afraid.

"Anything?" said Uncle Frank. His eyes were red and wet.

"I did what Momma Irene told me," I said. I had done what I was told to do and that was that. Now I could cry, too.

They were all running around, mad and screaming, and wouldn't stop. I knew it then. Everything was different now.

TWENTY-FIVE

Ruth

We were all behind the house when the call came, except for Weeza who was out for groceries. We heard it from Ellis, my husband. He was shaking when he pushed open the back door with his cane and stood there.

"They can't find Jacob—"

One of us said, "What?"

"Jacob's missing in Dalton," Ellis said, coming down to us. "He was to the . . . I don't know. He's not where he's supposed to be. He didn't come home. That girl couldn't tell me anything—"

"What the hell are you saying?" said Hershel, his face bunching up and rushing over to Ellis. I went between them.

I am Ruth, Hershel and Frank's mother, and all kinds of thoughts went through my mind then. Jacob out there somewhere?

"The police won't look for him," Ellis said, his mouth hanging open, unbelieving of what he was saying even though he had just heard it. "Someone get on the phone. Jacob's missing in Dalton."

"Who told you?" asked Hershel, taking Ellis by his shoulders.

"Who? It was Cora, the girl. But she doesn't know anything. She can barely talk she's so scared. It was last night—"

"Last night!" I said, my heart thumping. "When last night?"

Everyone was screaming and rushing around then.

"Why so long?" Hershel said. "Oh, my God, why so long to tell us? There are other damn telephones. If they let Jacob get taken, I'll go over there—"

"He has not been *taken*!" I screamed. "And no you won't do anything! Frank has been ripping himself up trying to find Jacob, who is just lost. I'm sure he has. He's my son and he loves Jacob. You know your brother—"

"My brother!"

"He must be crazy with worry," I said, "and doing everything he can to find him. And the police, too—"

"The police!" Hershel screamed. "I'll kill them, too, they don't look for my boy. They've probably done it. They killed my Jacob—"

"Stop, stop, stop!" I said, wanting to smack his face. "Stop all that before Weeza comes."

"The police!" he said again, mad as a wasp.

I held his arm strong. "The police," I repeated, trying to be calm. "Yes, they will be involved and will be looking for him. You think they want any trouble if they can avoid it? Everywhere a tinderbox? Everything in the papers? He is a boy lost and nothing more. You get yourself together, and you do it now, because it doesn't help anyone to hear you shouting like a crazy man. We need to get to Dalton right away."

Hershel stomped around the yard, whipping his head back and forth and cursing, and I told him again to be quiet. Then he rushed over to start the car but I knew there wasn't enough of it to start.

I went into the house to the telephone, when I saw Weeza come up the walk with two shopping bags. My heart went to ice. I ran down the steps and met her before she got to the house and told her, poor girl, I tried to tell her, but she got unsteady on her feet right away. Then her knees went weak and she fell in the yard. Apples rolled into the dust.

"Weeza!" said Ellis, dropping his cane and helping her up to the porch.

"Sit down," I said.

"I can't sit," she said right away. "We have to

go there!" Her hands shaking, her voice high, she trembling and trying to be calm. "We have to take the bus. It's the only way to get there. Hershel, get away from that damn car!" she yelled to the side yard. "Will someone call and find out the times?"

"What?" said Ellis, who was holding her hand and who loves Weeza and Jacob like his own. "What times, honey? What is it you mean?"

"Never mind, I'll call," Weeza said.

"I will," I said, trying to be firm. "I'll find out the bus times and ask Mrs. to drive us to the station. Somehow get word that we're coming. She'll do that for me."

At first Hershel didn't go to her, then he went to her, but it didn't do her any good to hear him say kill this and kill that. She closed his mouth with her hand and he tore himself away crazy. I didn't like that. Why do we have to coddle our men when we are torn up just as deep?

The car never did start. Hershel whipped the fenders with his hat and cut his fingers and cried and kicked the doors and lights and everything until he fell to the dust and had to be pulled away. Ellis tried to bring him into the house. The neighbors were all out by then. But Hershel wouldn't go in. He just stopped before the door, leaning hard against the post with his face sobbing in his arms until he slipped all the way to the porch floor. And Weeza trying not to, but she couldn't stop crying on the phone to the Atlanta police. They said they couldn't do anything about a child missing so far out of town, but all she said was "Jacob, Jacob, Jacob, my Jacob!"

TWENTY-SIX

Hershel

Weeza was on the phone back and forth for nearly an hour. I hated that car. There was nothing I would not do for my boy.

Jacob lying in a ditch somewhere by the side of the Dixie Road, his eyes staring at the sky? Oh, God in heaven. I cannot tell you. A boy was found last year, but you won't read it in any paper. And that man they just killed with his own shotgun and called it suicide. I read that lie. Or that poor boy in Money whose mother laid him out all open for everybody to see what they did to him. And thinking of our Jacob, his face like that, is a thing I cannot put out of my mind. There is no law for Negroes, marches or no marches, boycotts or no boycotts.

And maybe I know something about it.

Jacob didn't know what it meant when he said it. I'm sure he didn't. But if he ever said to someone else what he said to me, I don't know what would happen. He was with me when he said it, but if he wasn't? It makes me shake when I think of it.

"She's white top to bottom, isn't she, Poppa?"

When I heard him say it and saw his grin, I rose up inside like a devil because I knew he heard it from one of the older boys who think he is older, too, or don't care he isn't.

"Jacob!" I said, raising my hand so fast his grin went away.

When I took his face in my hand and pulled the other one back he was surprised and began to cry. I got ready to, but I didn't slap him. He said, "Poppa, Poppa, I'm sorry!" I told him to wipe that look from his face and those words from his mind and never say them again, ever, to anybody. How would he like it if a white man said that about his sister? If somebody said that kind of thing about Weeza? It's a dirty thing. It's just words but it's dirty. He wouldn't like it, I told him. It would be as nasty a thing as he ever heard. I wrapped his face in my hands and hoped he would learn something. Putting my mouth close to his ear I said, "Don't ever say that, Jacob, don't say that, please don't say that." He just looked at me, into my eyes, his little face, and then we were both crying. Weeza came in and asked what it was about. I was going to say something, but not the real reason, when Jacob got right up and went to Weeza and cried on her. At that second I saw how young Jacob is no matter how tall he is, and also how they love each other, and how good a boy he is.

I'm sure Weeza wanted to know what it was about, why we were sobbing. But she didn't ask again, just left us two by ourselves together.

I didn't hit Jacob that time, but there was another time and another hit. That first time, the boy was me. Frank was out and I tried to laugh and even though my daddy saw my scared eyes, his hand was already moving at my face and his mouth yelling, "Okay, Buster, it's you this time!"

The crying I did, and then my mother coming in. I saw how Daddy had to keep being mad, madder than he really was, to win her over to his side. He had to act as if his anger was bigger than my crying and my stung cheek. His anger had to be bigger than hers about him slapping me. He knocked things around, roared out of the house as if it was all him. That he was the only one who struggled to make our family work right, that our family was too big a thing to let go to the dogs, and it was only him stopping us from it. He didn't come back until Momma was sleeping but I was still awake, hating him. But I never thought about this, that Jacob would go and not come back. When I heard about Cora's telephone call, all the old thoughts came back to me and I hated my father again, but I cried for him, too.

Let me also tell you that Weeza screamed and said, "The ticket! The ticket!" and I said, "What?" and she said, "The ticket!" her eyes burning as if I didn't hear the word. So I said, "What ticket?" and she said, "He only gave us there, just there, and not back, as if the Lord knew Jacob didn't need a ticket home!" I didn't understand what she was saying. I don't think anybody understood what she was saying. But when she said she had to call her mother, then I came out with it.

"I told your mother to go away," I said.

Her face was all screwed up, tears rolling down her cheeks. "What—"

It all rushed out. "That day I took the train to Mobile to say we were getting married and ask her and Jacob to live with us," I said. "But she said no, she was moving to Ohio to be with her mother. So I said Jacob should stay with us, that you love him. And I do, too. She said no, he was her son. I said but I have a good job, and she laughed and said for how long, that I was my father's son. Then I got heated, and my words got loud, and I said she wouldn't take care of Jacob like we would. She swore at me and I did at her and she told me to get out and take Jacob with me, she wasn't coming back ever. Weeza, it was so easy for her to say Jacob should go with me that I knew I was right. She didn't want him as much as we do. That's why she's gone and why he's been our son these six years."

Weeza looked at me like I was talking nonsense, but I was crying and saying I was sorry I spoke to her mother like that, not because I wasn't right, but because I hurt Weeza. She shook her head over and over as if trying to rid herself of my words.

"Doesn't matter now," she said. "Doesn't matter now."

Even now, while Momma Ruth is getting us all together, Weeza just cries and won't let me near her. "Please," she says, "please just make something bad not happen this time," and I understand that well enough. She is talking about what happened to that boy four years ago. And all I can think of is his crushed face in that open box. I wanted to tell her how different that was, that Jacob would not end up in a box like that, but all I said was "I'm trying, I'm trying."

She says we must find Jacob or nothing will ever be right.

TWENTY-SEVEN

Bobby

N ot the bus," he said when they woke Friday morning in the motel room in Atlanta. "Not the bus, please."

"It's the cheapest way," said his mother coldly. "We can't afford to rent a car. The trains are on strike. I want this damn trip over. I'm sorry. I have to get home. I need to be home."

"Not the bus," said Bobby. "*She* can take one, but not us."

"Grandma *is* taking one, and so are we," she said, and slipped into the bathroom to dress. "Get your clothes on and pack."

This was wrong. This was bad. They were five hundred miles from their airplane, and the trains were on strike. They really ought to have the car to get back home, but now the car was wrecked. With three of them in there, there would have been plenty of room, and they could have driven straight through the night and been home by tomorrow night. In the car, if his brother was up front with the TripTik, he could have the whole backseat to lie down on. Not now. It was all wrong.

They'd stayed in a cheap motel near the railroad tracks, which was the only one they found after the Triple-A truck towed the wrecked car away. The motel had no pool. The car park was filled with junky cars. They'd had to use a taxi for everything since yesterday. Their mother was barely talking now, full of sharp looks, as Grandma walked onto the platform to take a bus south to St. Petersburg.

"I'm sorry," said their mother. "This has been a bust. I'm sorry about the car. About everything."

Grandma nodded. "Come visit me?"

"Of course," their mother said, looking away.

"Yes. You, too?" she said to the boys.

"Of course," repeated their mother, although Grandma was looking alternately at Bobby then Ricky then Bobby again.

Ricky said, "Sure," and hugged her.

"Sure," Bobby said, trying to smile, but Grandma looked down at him with her face pouching, not moving to hug him until a bus horn shattered the quiet. "My poor Bobchicka," she said finally, pressing her hand heavily on his shoulder. He watched her eyes, but they were deeper and farther away than before.

He felt his chest go empty when she walked up the steps into the silver bus and the driver pulled the door closed. That was it. A few minutes later, the bus left the terminal, coughing and squealing away into the white air.

"She'll be home by tonight," their mother said, pulling her eyes away from the blurry street. "I have to deal with insurance now, then we'll be out of this terrible place by lunchtime."

Poor Bobchicka. His grandmother couldn't bring herself to hug him.

She was letting him go.

Two hours later they were back at the bus terminal, heaving their suitcases out of a hot taxicab onto the hotter sidewalk. Bobby was headed toward the door behind his mother when she dropped her luggage on the sidewalk and swung around. "Give it to me," she said.

"What?"

"You know what. That damn stick!"

"I . . ." he started, moving his hand toward his pants pocket, but not putting it in. "I lost it."

Faster than he imagined she could, she drove her hand into the same front pocket. Finding it empty, she searched the others, front and back, roughly.

"I lost it," he repeated.

"Don't *ever* let me see one of those things again. You hear me? *Ever.* And if you *ever* steal anything again, so help me, I will make you regret it for the rest of your life." She looked as if she would hit him, she looked as cold as his father had, but also hurt. Staring at him with dark eyes, then taking her eyes off him as if something between them had broken, she turned on her heels, grabbed her bags, and walked up the sidewalk to the station.

Ricky had watched every moment of this from a few feet off, his eyes narrowing to little slits behind his glasses. He didn't move.

"What?" said Bobby.

"It's so easy, isn't it?" said Ricky.

"What's easy?"

"To be lucky," said Ricky. "It's so easy to be lucky."

"What are you talking about?"

"You've always been lucky. You could have just said nothing. About the bullet. You could have just said nothing."

"What do you mean?" asked Bobby.

"So stupid easy," he said, and right there he dropped the souvenir slug he had found in the dirt at Lookout Mountain. It rolled to the edge of the sidewalk and off into the gutter. Without looking,

he walked toward the station, his book-laden suitcase knocking his knee with every step.

Was that it? Was Bobby lucky? Was that all it
was? Could he so easily have been in his brother's
shoes? Was there only a thread of a difference between them, after all? Brothers. Nearly the same age.
Interchangeable? Could Ricky's bad eyes have been
his bad eyes? Was that why Ricky was taken to Indians games? Because of what might happen? And
yet Bobby had been vicious to him, saying things
that couldn't be taken back. So now, one by one,
his grandmother, his mother, and now Ricky had
stepped away from him.

"Get in. Get in here!" his mother said, kicking
open the door to the station, pushing herself
through, then letting it fall closed on Ricky as Bobby
watched from the gutter.

So that was it, after all. That he didn't know, that
he was mixed up, that he made nothing but mistakes, that he could steal and be mean and be angry,
that he could look around at everything and know
things were broken and wrong and unfair and not
know what to do or say to fix them, except to grunt
and run like an animal.

That was it, that was all he could do, that was
who he was.

Bobby dragged his red suitcase across the sidewalk

after his brother, through the door, and across the floor of the big foul-smelling room, trembling, sick to his stomach, his legs tingling from his ankles to his bottom as if someone were spying at him from a high hidden place.

TWENTY-EIGHT

The terminal smelled of coffee and sweat and exhaust and it echoed with the sound of voices from every direction. The long room was half waiting room, half lunchroom, with a low wall separating the benches and booths and a bank of windows overlooking the bus platform, which was no more than a raised sidewalk under a low roof.

Several buses were outside, parked at an angle to the building. On the flank of each was the famous image of the lean racing dog, promising fast bus travel. The buildings beyond the roof were white in the sun. The street shimmered with heat.

The two boys sat silently at a booth while their mother bought tickets at a counter window under a clock that read five after eleven. When she returned with papers in her hand, she said she had purchased the last tickets and they were allowed to load their things onto the bus before they ate, though it wouldn't leave for almost an hour. Without a word about it, Ricky and his mother found a seat together on the bus. Bobby put his suitcase on the bench in front of them, but after they descended the steps, he decided to move it to the one behind.

Bobby hated the big hot dirty city and wanted only to be home, though thinking now of their small house and his smaller room, with his brother and mother everywhere, and maybe his father home from Washington, he wasn't sure it would be better than here or anywhere else.

He settled his hands on the lunch table. The sandwich his mother put before him was dry. When had it been made? By whom? By black hands? The black hands at the car window. His own hand on the crank, keeping his window sealed. The car's insane twisting away from the shack. And now the sudden smell of cigarettes and dirty underwear as a couple of men slumped into the booth next to them. The more he thought about it, the more he felt he was going to throw up.

The wall clock's wide face stared ahead, unconcerned.

There was still close to an hour before the bus left and even then it made stops every half hour. Racing dog? That was wrong. The bus was just standing there! Their suitcases were already on it. Why couldn't *they* get on it and just leave? His mother said they were lucky to get tickets at all, she had to pay extra to get them and now the bus was full because of the train strike. When he remembered the airplane, it made him sick all over again how the trip was ending this way. He wanted only to be home. Or anywhere but here.

The man behind the ticket counter glanced slowly around the room at the people eating, then slid a sign over the window and walked slowly into another room.

"When is our bus going to leave?" Bobby asked his mother, knowing the answer, but wanting to show how bored he was, and wasn't there something she could do? But she didn't answer his question. She was reading a newspaper someone had left on the lunch table. The ticket man returned. The clock had barely moved.

She put the paper down. "Boys, I want to warn . . ." She paused, ruffling the newspaper. "Never mind. Nothing."

"Mom?" said Ricky.

She didn't look up from the newspaper that she kept lining up with the edge of the table. Bobby's mind swam with the headlines. "Manhunt . . . Negro Youth . . . Prophet . . . Rape . . . Shotgun . . . White Teenager . . ."

"Nothing," she said finally. "It's raining at home.

Oh, and Daddy will be there when we get back. That's all."

So that was it. His father was waiting at home. She'd tried to hide it by saying it casually, but that's what she was warning them about. He was mad again. Even home was not a place to be.

More minutes of silence.

Bobby shivered in the heat. "When is our bus going to leave?" he asked stupidly.

His mother shot a look at the clock on the wall. "We can board in thirty minutes. A little less. Don't you have to go to the bathroom?"

"No."

He was worried that if he saw a toilet he would have to throw up, and he didn't want to. At least the bus would be moving, air would come in on them. It would be hot air, but it would be moving. He needed to get out of there. He was a thief. He was mean. He was lucky and he had no right to be. He hated his hitting father. He hated history and the Civil War. He was dumb and unfinished, a dirty little boy, and everyone in the room, everyone everywhere, knew it. He counted the lines on the schedule. Thirteen stops from Atlanta to Cleveland. Two days. It would never end. They would never get back home. He would be sick and would never see his room again. He hated the room he shared with his brother, and his father would be there, typing in the den, ready to burst out, but there was nowhere else for Bobby to go.

He wondered if the bathroom was occupied in case he had to vomit. There it was, the men's room, and it said WHITE over the door. He thought of what he did in there and none of it seemed white. He thought of the smell from the motel bathroom when his mother was in it. He saw another door through the partition. COLORED.

The schedule again. His vision was darkening, as if he were staring out light-headed from under a deep hood. The first stop was what? Marietta. Then Dalton then Chattanooga. He hated Chattanooga. The name sounded like someone vomiting. His armpits were souring with smell. Down on the list was a stop called Cleveland, only it was Cleveland, Tennessee. And if they called another city Cleveland, you could bet it was far away from the real Cleveland. They would never get home. Never. All the miles ahead. Two days of miles.

Heat began to creep up the sides of his face from his neck to the top of his scalp, and his cheeks burned, while his whole head now felt suddenly chill and heavy. He breathed in, but the air in the room was close and foul and thickly warm.

He lowered his nose into his glass and breathed in the plain no-scent of tepid water. It didn't help. Running his hand over his damp scalp he felt his hair bristle. A shiver ran down his spine. Was he going to pass out? He slid out of the booth and stole across the room, trying with every fiber not to vomit or faint.

"Bobby—"

He didn't answer, but pushed quickly through the restroom door. When he entered its coolness—he guessed it had been empty for some minutes because it didn't smell like he expected—the burning in his stomach and face lessened. He closed himself in a wooden stall and waited. Looking down into the bowl, but not leaning toward it, he felt nothing, not even the urge to pee. Good. He might not be sick after all.

Outside the stall, he ran his hands under the cold water and splashed his face. That was better. There were no towels, cloth or paper, so he dried his cheeks on his shirt shoulders and stood staring at his face in the mirror. He hated the fat dumb thing. His eyes were pale green and weak. Not weak of vision, but of the thing that made eyes truthful. He remembered his father's eyes when he slapped him for crying. He hated those weak eyes, too, but forget them. His face in the mirror now was mean and weak in its own way. He was a shape of dough, a blob, a thing unfinished, still waiting to be made. He was empty, unfilled.

His hands were dry now. He turned.

The door pushed in at him, and a big black shape with deep brown eyes stepped nearly on top of him. Bobby froze, there was nowhere to go, and felt the heat rise in his cheeks again and in the hollow of his throat. Beyond the shape, in the waiting room outside, he saw his mother standing. "Bobby," she said quietly.

"If you're done," said the big black man, and he pushed past Bobby and entered the stall with a groan.

"Sorry, Mom," he said when they were outside. "I'm sorry. I didn't see the sign."

"Finish your sandwich," she said. "It's almost time."

TWENTY-NINE

When he sat again, he felt Ricky's eyes on him but didn't return the look. He imagined an expression of amusement or anger.

The sandwich was tasteless. Taking a small bite, Bobby turned to see the uniformed man move back from the counter window, his face hidden for a moment as he worked on things behind him. The sound of papers and something ticking.

Footsteps at the street door. Bobby looked out to see a long yellow car drive away and, as if it were possible, felt more heat pour through the door from the white air outside. The ticket man looked up from what he was working on. The ticking stopped.

A brown man eased into the room with them. He wore a dark brimmed hat set a little to the side. He stepped into the waiting room as if he knew everyone was looking at him. Bobby wondered why the man hadn't entered the bus station through the door that said COLORED WAITING ROOM over it. He would have to, wouldn't he?

"There was a sign," the brown man said to the ticket man. "At the colored window. It's closed now."

"Be with you in a few minutes," said the ticket man, turning back to his work. "Please wait on the street until I call for you."

"Sir, we telephoned before and hurried to get here in time to catch—"

The white man looked up. "Until I *call* for you. You're not hard of hearing, are you, son?"

"No, sir," the brown man said, stopping.

"I thought not. Please? Outside?"

The man tipped his hat slightly and stepped backward through the doorway to the sidewalk outside. Bobby watched the others move to him. Were they a family? Some were very black. Some were regular. There were two women, one younger than his mother, one older, then the man with the hat, and an older man, with short gray hair, leaning on a cane. They stayed in a cluster outside, until the older woman leaned to the window to read the chalkboard schedule over the top of Bobby's head. The younger man with the hat took a step up behind her and looked over her shoulder at the schedule. They were so close to him now.

The young woman stood a bit apart from the

others. Her skin was like light coffee. She seemed to Bobby as if she were afraid, her eyes darting at everything, settling on nothing, always moving. The lunchroom window was open and he heard their low quiet talk.

The older man, wearing dark pants and a dark shirt and beige vest, half unbuttoned, appeared in the doorway. His skin was blacker than the younger man's. Bobby felt his neck stiffen.

"Is that the same man?" he whispered to Ricky.

"Who?" his brother said, turning to the window.

"That one."

"Same as who?"

"The old man at the shack when Mom crashed into the garbage can and he came out and we took off. Isn't it the same man?"

"Him?" said his brother. He adjusted his glasses, blinked several times through them, looked closely at the older man. For a moment it seemed their eyes met. He looked away. "You're nuts."

"It sure looks like him."

"You're completely nuts. This one's taller than the guy who came out of the house. And younger."

Maybe, but Bobby couldn't stop looking at the family. They weren't like the chocolate men on his street. They were so much closer, for one thing. They talked softly to one another, moving their hands. The words were too low for him to make out.

He looked at the schedule again, saw again how many stops there were before reaching Ohio, and his throat tightened.

There were footsteps on the platform outside. The young brown man was striding down the platform ahead of the others. The short older black woman walked past the platform door, a heavy oak door with a glass window, carrying a cloth shopping bag in each hand. The one in her right hand bulged with something and caught the door on her way past. It made a sound. Then the four of them were together at the open door of the waiting bus. Then they walked up the steps into it.

"What?" Bobby whispered. His chest spiked.

He saw the four shapes inside the bus pass down the aisle and sit down in seats near the window. The man with the hat took his hat off.

"Mom, that's our bus," Bobby whispered. "Those people took our seats." He tugged her arm. "Mom, they took our seats. Our stuff is in there. My suitcase is right there. That's our seats. You said it would be safe—"

His mother rose from the table, her face paling. She glanced over at the ticket man, but he had already dropped what he was doing and leaned over the counter toward the platform door. "Hey. No, no," he said. "No, no. You can't—"

"Hey!" A louder voice this time.

It was the driver of the bus, who had been smoking at the counter with a cup of coffee in front of him. Now he twisted around, and now he was up off the stool. "Hey, get outta there!" he said, moving quickly through the tables toward the door, trailing cigarette smoke behind him. He jumped up the bus steps and yelled loud enough for the lunchroom to hear, shooing the family out of their seats like cats. "No you don't. No you don't. That's . . . we have whites on this bus. We're full up. This ain't no sit-in. Get offa here—"

The family was on the platform again, and his mother sat back down.

"You don't understand, sir," Bobby heard the younger man say as he followed the driver into the lunchroom, but stepped back just inside the platform door, holding his hat. "You see, sir," he started, when the ticket seller stepped out from behind the counter and in one, two, three steps, he was there and slipped behind the man, blocking the way to the platform. The brown man turned toward him suddenly, his mouth open, but saying nothing. The ticket seller watched the man's hand reach for the knob on the door to the platform, and he slapped the brown hand away from the knob.

It was not a hard slap, and the ticket seller seemed as surprised as the man whose hand he had slapped.

The room went quiet, and no one moved. On

the platform beyond the windows the young woman trembled on her feet, one hand over her mouth, watching the three men.

Bobby knew she was afraid of something about to happen. He felt his neck turn cold and clammy.

The young man lowered his head and repeated, "Yes, sir, but you don't understand, sir—"

"What don't I understand, *sir*?" the ticket man said, no longer surprised at the slap but looking now as if he might do it again.

"It's about our Jacob—"

"That's not your bus," the driver said. "That's this people's bus," he said, waving his hand into the lunchroom. "They paid for their seats, and the bus is full because of the strike. Maybe you heard of the railroad strike where you come from?"

"Yes, sir, I've heard of it, but you see we called about seats, and they said—"

"They are going back up north, and their seats are on that bus, which is full because of the strike."

"I know about the strike, sir," the brown man said. "But we need to get to Dalton because our son is missing—"

A smirk on the driver's face. "You all have the same son now?"

"No, sir. *My* son. We called before. And Mrs. called. She talked to you, and there are seats—"

The ticket man was almost laughing now. "I don't know who your Mrs. is, but this bus is full," he said. "Didn't you hear us? You can't get on *this* bus. You can take the *next* bus. It leaves in three hours. You know what three hours is?"

"But we have seats for now—"

"This—bus—is—full!"

Ricky stood up from the table and stared at the three men.

He stood up and stared and stepped toward the men.

The room went electric with dark eyes. All the people at the other tables turned from looking at the group of men to look at this boy who stood up. No one spoke. Bobby was sitting right next to him but didn't stand. Ricky took two steps toward the brown man, the ticket man, and the driver. He didn't even look like he wanted to, but that's what his body made him do. Just the movement, the only thing in the lunchroom to move, and his face, his shiny glasses, looking directly at what was happening, made the men pause. The two white men turned their attention to him.

Ricky took another step.

Bobby didn't know what his brother was doing.

From across the room, the ticket man waved his finger at Ricky as if marking the figure "1" on a chalkboard. His mouth was open, his features twisted as if he were going to object, but he said nothing, just marked the air at his brother's face.

Bobby understood. The man wanted his brother to sit down.

What happened next was that a door opened and a man in a blue cap appeared from an office behind the counter. He must have heard the raised voices. Ricky kept looking at the men by the door, not sitting down, poised as if to take another step, his back heel lifted off the floor, but not taking the step. His mother stared at her son, her face dumbstruck.

"Ricky, sit down—"

"No," he said softly.

Bobby glanced up at the clock, at the lunch tables, at the brown faces on the platform looking at the younger man, then at the clock, then at the man's face, then at his brother's face.

The man in the conductor's cap wove through the tables to the group at the door. "So . . ." he began.

He spoke quietly to all of them one after another, talked over their talking, quietly, insistently, listened to the two white men, then to the brown man, then to the older woman with the bags, which she had not put down when she came in from the platform, and suddenly there was a clipboard now. The older woman was crying solemnly, softly, though Bobby heard her drawing huge wet breaths, and using her arms to help her talk. It was musical when she spoke. Bobby glanced beyond their little group to the bus steps and the younger woman with skin like coffee marked by streaks of tears. Her face just then was one he could imagine watching the Lincoln train pass in the night. She held her hands close to her mouth almost as if she were praying, just as she might have when the wind-stirred bunting drew by. Watching her, even for a second or two, he felt the blood drain from his face as if he had done something wrong to look at her, and he had to turn away.

The ticket man was pointing his thumb over his shoulder at the easel or the clock, saying, "But the later bus at three—"

"But you see . . ." the man with the hat in his hands said. And the word "Dalton" came out again. And the name "Jacob."

The conductor hushed the ticket man gently and, as he spoke, put one hand on the brown man's sleeve. The brown man did not move his arm from under the white man's hand, but turned to the young woman, who was inside the lunchroom now, and she to him. Her face was like polished stone in the rain, her eyes full of crying, but her mouth was closed and her chin up.

"So," the man with the cap said finally, pulling away from the group. He then tugged something from his pocket. It was a watch. He went to one lunch table, then to another, and a third, nodding here and there, speaking quietly and using his hands as he spoke. After approaching a fifth table, he said, "Thank you . . ."

Ricky, who had been stock-still, relaxed a little now. He didn't move forward or back, just relaxed; his heel touched the floor.

"Sit down," said his mother. "Ricky, sit down. Your sandwich. Sit down." He didn't. He watched the group by the door.

The conductor faced the room. "We're going to start boarding now," he said over the tables, looking at Bobby and his family, at their plates, their food, at the others. "We're going to start boarding now."

THIRTY

The third man had done this: found a couple and a single man and woman alone who agreed to take the later bus. The remaining passengers would move up, and there would be room for the black family in the rear. The third man had worked it out to find four seats for them.

Once in his proper seat, his suitcase on the rack above him, Bobby hoped that the incident with the Negro passengers was over. The Negro passengers, he thought, as he rehearsed his telling of the story to the Downings next door. He wouldn't call them chocolate this time, though he wondered why they needed to be on that particular bus and what the end of the story would be. Sitting sideways and glancing back, he saw the two men, looking afraid and angry, whisper to each other, while the older woman fussily arranged her bags at her feet. The younger one sat between them, her eyes staring blankly ahead, unable to stay dry.

When it finally roared alive and left the terminal, the bus was beyond hot, a tin box of old heat. And there was the bad smell of human gas floating past him every few minutes. Bobby tried to guess who the offender was, but no one looked back as if they cared who was smelling what, so he leaned his face against the open window to catch what fresher air there might have been, but the bus rolled through one hot street after another as slowly as the old Chrysler had moved through the streets near his home the day they left.

THIRTY-ONE

Hershel

S ing," she said in my ear after a half hour of no words.

I turned to her. "I can't sing. I won't sing. Don't ask me to."

"You better do something. Your wife needs to hear from you, and if it won't be talking, it better be singing."

Momma Ruth put her eyes on me and wouldn't take them off me. She was steaming. I didn't know what to do. I didn't want to talk. I was so mad. I was still shaking from the bus station. That man who struck my hand from that doorknob. And me thanking him yes, sir, yes, sir, and wanting to kick him till he didn't move.

"Damn Jacob's whistling and his gawking! He's just a damn boy who should have known his place—"

"Shut your mouth!" Ruth said, closing her hand on my lips.

I pushed it away. I knew it was Frank who had allowed it to happen. He always did things wrong. He messed things up. Or maybe it wasn't Frank, but I had to be mad at somebody and he was easy to be mad at, and then I regretted thinking that. I hoped against everything that Jacob was not in a ditch by some road, but I kept seeing that open box, and his little dead face in it, and my heart shook with crying. I tried not to do it out loud but Momma Ruth knew what was going on in me.

"Stop that now," she said, patting my hands. "We're waiting."

That bus was quiet! No one saying a word.

I went in my head through all the songs I knew and they wouldn't work except in a jook house, until I went back to when I was a boy. In my head I heard some words from a long time ago. I didn't know how right they were, but I started humming the tune, then I spoke out the words I remembered. When they all started coming back to me, I sang them, but low at first.

Life crushes me with burdens
I tremble, stumble down
My Lord, He lifts my head up
There to set a starry crown.

THIRTY-TWO

Bobby

How after all that, Bobby had gotten an empty seat for just himself, he didn't know, but he sat leaning against the window, and saw for the first time a small sign over the seat two rows ahead of him. It read: COLORED. It took him a moment to realize that it probably said WHITE on the other side, and that he, Ricky, and his mother were in the the colored section.

He turned his head slightly. The young woman was bent over, fussing with the older one's bags. Her hands trembled and quaked as if she was sick. Her face wouldn't stop being wet. The older man had his hand on her shoulder, patting it.

Bobby was damp all over. The dusty-hot streets, the window heat, the noon sun coming from straight up there, from the crest of the sky, moving its whiteness along the aisle floor whenever the bus turned. He hated filthy dusty Atlanta, its crawling traffic, he hated the South, hated himself, wanted not to be in his own skin anymore or be anywhere at all. But here he was in the suffocating heat of a slow-moving iron box. All around him the passengers were hushed. No one spoke except in whispers, probably about what had happened at the station, all of which made it easy to hear when one of the men began to hum, then hum with his mouth open, then sing.

Our journey may be weary
Our ride to heaven long

The driver glanced up into the mirror and asked him to please quiet down, and the brown man did for a while, but his voice grew louder once more, as if he couldn't help it, and this time the driver said nothing.

There was something about the way the man sang that was full of pain, like tugging raw nerves out of the dirt. His voice coiled and twisted, lingered on a word, stopped short, then came up again. Soon, the other brown people began talking while he sang. Or, not talking, but humming along or speaking out isolated words that may or may not have been the words to the song.

Bobby leaned forward and whispered, "What's it all about?"

His brother's face was pressed to the window ahead of his. "I think somebody died. Probably somebody they know died."

When Bobby glanced over his shoulder, the singing man's eyes were closed, with the young woman's head bent to his shoulder, her cheeks still wet behind a handkerchief. The song was about burdens and crushing and resting and dying, and his chest felt both hollow and full at the same time and he wanted to cry, too. What was going on?

Had someone really died?

He decided someone *had* died.

So it was with him wherever he was. He began to feel as if, no longer the death train or the death car, now the bus carried a coffin among them. It rumbled down the road, looking like a bus, squealing and stirring up dust like a bus, but was not a bus, for inside it a box draped in bunting and black crape was rising from beneath the floor of the aisle, up and up, until it stopped between the seats for all to see. Who was inside? Not Lincoln. Not his grandfather. Then who? Whose casket was it?

And the song went on.

Lord, leadeth me unto my throne
Where I shall rest when day is done

The man's voice washed over the death box like a wave taking all of them with it, from the backseats where they sat, up to the front, including the driver, who said nothing even though the sound was louder than ever. Bobby's eyes stung with the idea that this brown family, who had nearly been refused seats on his bus, was approaching in the town of Dalton a death that they dreaded so deeply but just as deeply could not avoid.

His chest was a thing of lead. The coffin lid pressed heavily on it. And the song went on and on.

Our journey may be weary
Our ride to heaven long.

THIRTY-THREE

They drove all the roads to Dalton listening to that song, then to a second one that sounded much like it, then to none at all, the not-sound of which was like its own song rolling and rolling.

In that silence that wasn't silence, the fantastic coffin kept growing. It grew larger and larger until it took up the entire bus and they were all inside it, the not-song washing over them and over them. Bobby couldn't breathe, the way you can't breathe when your head is out the car window and the air pushes into your nose and suffocates you.

Ricky said nothing. Their mother was in her own place now, private and shadowed, the olive circles under her eyes as dark as Bobby had ever seen them. The bus rolled along the road neither too slowly nor too quickly, but gravely and with respect for the re-alities of street traffic, like its own funeral procession, a coffin on wheels rolling correctly road to road in the oppressive heat.

Almost two hours after the bus started, Bobby saw the town sign: DALTON, 3 MI.

A sharp yell from behind him and the tumbling of heavy bags.

"Hold your horses back there," the driver rasped when both women jumped up from their seats and the young one came a few steps up the aisle and halted next to Bobby's seat, hunched over and searching with her eyes out the windshield. He smelled the smell of laundry detergent from her dress. Her hand was on the seat back in front of him.

"Down, please," the driver said, slowing. "Sit down."

The women didn't sit but clung to the seat backs, which the driver saw in the rearview mirror, but he didn't say anything else. It was the same as when he told the man to quiet the singing. They didn't sit, as if they couldn't sit, like Ricky didn't sit, and the driver didn't say any more.

The young woman's hand didn't move from the seat rest, inches from Bobby's face. She couldn't have been very old. Her hand was smooth and small and holding tightly to the iron bar of the seat back.

He thought of the ash can his mother had crumpled and the ash cans on his street in Cleveland and the hands of those men and the hand of this woman and he thought of the word, *that* word, and was ashamed of it.

He felt his chest heave and his throat sting and his own hand move—his hand, with its knuckles still nicked from scraping sticks. He watched his hand move, cross up before his eyes to the woman's hand. He watched it settle over her warm fingers lightly, like a cloth settling over them. She looked down at him and his hand with surprise, her lips opening, but she did not remove her hand from under his. He molded his little white fingers to the shape of hers, but lightly, searching her face to see if she was already changing, the way he worried his mother had changed when his grandfather had died. Her eyes looked on him, wide and open. He couldn't tell what she was thinking, but he did not move his fingers. He knew Ricky was staring at him and at his hand, but he could not take it away.

There was a sound ahead, a yell or a call, and the bus jerked. Bobby's hand was still on the young woman's. It was there for a minute, perhaps two, until the bus jerked again, and she softly withdrew her fingers, meeting his eyes again for an instant, then twisting her face in a gasp at what she saw out the windshield.

Peering to the front now, Bobby saw two police cars, black-and-white sedans, parked at angles, with a red fez light on each roof, but not flashing, and their sirens silent. The older woman standing behind the younger one groaned, fell to her knees in the aisle, and started to cry. "Oh, he's gone!" When the bus wobbled up to the brick building, Bobby saw on his right a brown woman appear in the open doorway from inside the station, her wide-eyed look jumping from one rear window to the next. She met his eyes for an instant, too. Her face was wet, she was heaving, sobbing, barely able to stand, and his chest throbbed.

"Oh, my God, it's Olivia!" said the man who had sung.

Out of the dark station doorway came a man who so looked like the singing man on the bus it could have been his twin. He clutched the woman's shoulders, also searching the bus windows one after another, also crying.

Behind Bobby, the whole family was in the aisle now, sobbing out a jumble of voices. The bus slowed to a crawl. Two police officers stood next to the black couple on the platform, their faces unseen in the shadows of their hat brims.

The young woman next to Bobby sank to her knees and wailed. The man with the hat bent to her, making sounds in his throat. Bobby smelled him, too. He smelled the same as his own sweat, sour and afraid.

The instant the bus stopped at the curb, the family lurched for the door to get out before anyone else. All the white people stayed in their seats, as if strapped to them. The older woman left her bags on the floor below the seat, yelling at the top of her lungs.

Then the woman on the platform outside started shaking her head. "No, no, no!" she sobbed. Then there was movement behind her, and an older black woman with gray hair appeared on the platform with her arms around the shoulders of a young boy.

The boy wobbled in the darkness of the doorway. When the bus door gasped open, he raised his head at the young woman stumbling down the steps. His face was streaming as wet as hers.

"Oh, my God!" the young woman cried. "Jacob! Jacob! Jacob!"

"It was Frank—" someone called out.

The boy's face crumbled when he ran to the young woman whose hand Bobby had touched. Screaming, she flew to him at the same time and wrapped her arms around him and pressed him into her as if to never let him go.

"Frank found him," someone said. "He searched and searched. He was lost, just—"

"Ja—cob! Ja—cob!" the older woman screamed now from the bus steps, falling to her knees in the dusty road, while the older man behind her nearly tripped onto the sidewalk, then bent down to help her to her feet.

"Jacob—" The younger man leaped out the door in a rush, falling onto the sidewalk. His hat rolled off in a wide half circle. It seemed as if he fell on his face, but he picked himself right up and lunged to the station's open doorway.

The young woman sobbed—"Jacob! Jacob!"—melting again and again into his little arms and she and the boy faltered, but the hatless man was there to hold her up, hold them both up, his chin shaking like hers and the boy's. The three of them wrapped themselves together in a moving ball of brown faces and arms.

The two white boys and their mother and everyone watched from their seats on the bus, saying nothing.

Also saying nothing, the driver made his way down the aisle checking left and right. He carried the forgotten bags to the front, then handed them down, stood back on the bus steps, and watched the scene unfold on the station platform.

It went for minutes like this before the driver settled himself into his seat again and, checking his watch and looking in the mirror at the passengers, pulled the knobbed arm that closed the door with a hush, then threw the bus into gear. It shrieked and coughed a cloud of gray smoke over the sidewalk and began to move.

"Chattanooga next," he said. "Thirty-five minutes."

Ricky removed his glasses and pinched his eyelids shut. "I can't wait to be home."

Bobby said nothing while the wailing from the station continued to bubble in through the windows. His heart pounded against his ribs as the wet faces and arms wrapped around one another. Not able to take his eyes from them, he watched them teeter together on the platform, watched them stumble step by step together into the shadow of the station doorway, and watched them still as the bus drove up the long street, rolling heavily through the dust, until it turned the corner and, huffing for breath as if breathing was no longer possible, he couldn't see them anymore.

Author's Note

This story began with memories: my grandmother, mother, brother, and I did take such a battlefield tour in June 1959, and we witnessed several instances of Jim Crow in action, both among ourselves and more publicly in the South. Many parts of this novel are reflections of that trip. Since, however, my memories formed only a fragmentary narrative, other parts of the present story are necessarily fictional.

The system of racist customs and laws known as Jim Crow existed in varying degrees in the Southern states from roughly the fall of Reconstruction in 1877 to the Civil Rights and Voting Rights acts of 1964 and 1965. It was, in effect, a continuation of the slavery that had been abolished by the Emancipation Proclamation in 1863 and over which the Civil War had been fought. Jim Crow, named after an early nineteenth-century minstrel song, was pervasive, a way of life that governed every public action of African Americans in the South. They were not allowed to mix with whites in restaurants, railroad cars, buses, waiting rooms, theaters, restrooms, water fountains, parks, and pools. Factories, stores, banks, and other institutions had elaborate rules governing the intermingling of the races.

The realities of life under Jim Crow have been well documented, and some recent and widely available books include *Sons of Mississippi*, by Paul Hendrickson; *The Race Beat*, by Gene Roberts and Hank Klibanoff; *The Promised Land*, by Nicholas Lemann; *Trouble in Mind*, by Leon F. Litwack; and *There Goes My Everything*, by Jason Sokol. An essential volume of oral history transcripts (and audio recordings) of victims of the period is *Remembering Jim Crow*, edited by William H. Chafe, Raymond Gavins, and Robert Korstad, among others. *Sweet Land of Liberty*, by Thomas J. Sugrue, addresses, as its subtitle states, "the forgotten struggle for civil rights in the North." Richard Wright's 1937 autobiographical sketch, "The Ethics of Living Jim Crow," has not been surpassed.

In *Lunch-Box Dream*, Hershel Thomas refers several times to the 1955 killing in Money, Mississippi, of fourteen-year-old Emmett Till. Emmett lived in Chicago and was visiting relatives in Mississippi when he allegedly whistled at a white woman.

He was later kidnapped and his body recovered in the Tallahatchie River, identifiable only by his ring. To document the brutality of his murder, Emmett's mother displayed his body in a glass-topped coffin and allowed now-famous images to be published in *Ebony* magazine. By their own later admission, the white woman's husband and a relative had in fact killed Emmett, but had already been acquitted by the (usual for the time) all-white jury. The publicity surrounding Emmett Till's death, his funeral in Chicago, and the subsequent trial in Mississippi, strengthened immeasurably the civil rights movement in both the North and the South.

As a side note, Emmett's coffin was rediscovered in 2009 in a shed at the Chicago cemetery where he was buried and is now in the possession of the National Museum of African American History and Culture in Washington, D.C. Further information about the shotgun death Hershel refers to in chapter 26 can be found in the *Atlanta Journal-Constitution* from that week in June 1959.

I want to thank several friends who read this story at various times in its development and who offered many insightful comments and comfort, too: Nora, Elise, Dennis, Pat, Tami (thanks, also, for the photo of El Siesta), Karen, and Floyd. Thank you to Sarah Salomon, whom I do not know but who read the manuscript at a crucial stage. From the very beginning of my work on this book, my wife, Dolores, has been my conscience, inspiration, and sounding board. I am as ever grateful to my unstoppable agent, George Nicholson, for just that, not stopping until he found the perfect editor—Frances Foster, whose intelligence, grace, and imagination at our first meeting told me my story had found its true home. Every encounter since then has been a joy. Thanks are due also to Susan Dobinick, whose careful shepherding of the manuscript has made me long to stay at that new home for a good while to come.